THE GREAT
RABBIT
Rescue

Katie Davies

Illustrated by Hannah Shaw

Beach Lane Books

New York London Toronto Sydney New Delhi

MY VILLAGE
by Anna.

The Vet's

church

Sweet Shop

Pet Shop

TO JOE'S DADS APARTMENT

Railway Station

River

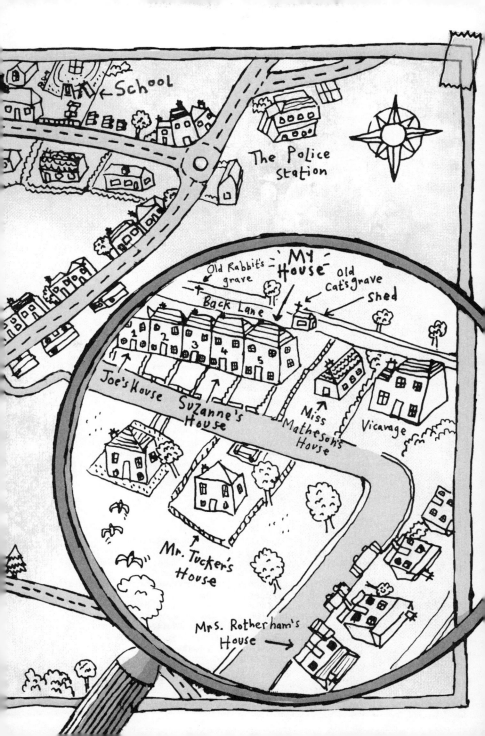

For Sam

Thanks to my Mum and Dad, and to my husband,
Alan, for reading (and reading) it.
And thanks also to my agent, Clare Conville, and to
Venetia Gosling and everyone at Simon and Schuster.

BEACH LANE BOOKS
An imprint of Simon & Schuster Children's Publishing Division
1230 Avenue of the Americas, New York, New York 10020
This book is a work of fiction. Any references to historical events, real people,
or real locales are used fictitiously. Other names, characters, places, and incidents
are products of the author's imagination, and any resemblance to actual events
or locales or persons, living or dead, is entirely coincidental.
Text copyright © 2010 by Katie Davies
Illustrations copyright © 2010 by Hannah Shaw
Originally published in Great Britain in 2010 by Simon and Schuster UK Ltd.
Published by arrangement with Simon and Schuster UK Ltd.
First U.S. edition 2011
All rights reserved, including the right of reproduction in whole or in part in any form.
BEACH LANE BOOKS is a trademark of Simon & Schuster, Inc.
For information about special discounts for bulk purchases, please contact Simon & Schuster
Special Sales at 1-866-506-1949 or business@simonandschuster.com.
The Simon & Schuster Speakers Bureau can bring authors to your live event. For more
information or to book an event, contact the Simon & Schuster Speakers Bureau at
1-866-248-3049 or visit our website at www.simonspeakers.com.
Manufactured in the United States of America
1111 FFG
First Edition
2 4 6 8 10 9 7 5 3 1
Library of Congress Cataloging-in-Publication Data
Davies, Katie, 1978–
The great rabbit rescue / Katie Davies ; illustrated by Hannah Shaw.—1st U.S. ed.
p. cm.
Summary: When Joe goes to live with his father across town and must leave behind
his beloved pet rabbit, his friends Anna and Suzanne try to take care of it for him,
but when the rabbit becomes ill and then Joe follows suit, the girls are certain
that both will die unless they are reunited.
ISBN 978-1-4424-2064-9 (hardcover)—ISBN 978-1-4424-3321-2 (eBook)
[1. Rabbits as pets—Fiction. 2. Sick—Fiction. 3. Friendship—Fiction.]
I. Shaw, Hannah, ill. II. Title.
PZ7.D283818Gs 2012
[Fic]—dc22
2011008326

❥ CHAPTER 1 ❥
A Real Rescue

This is a story about Joe-down-the-street, and why he went away, and how he got rescued. Most stories I've read about people getting rescued aren't *Real-Life* Stories. They're Fairy Stories, about Sleeping Beauty, and Rapunzel, and people like that. And they probably aren't true, because in Real Life people don't prick their fingers on spindles very much and fall asleep for a hundred years. And if they did, they probably wouldn't wake up just because someone gave them a kiss on the cheek, like Sleeping Beauty did. Even if the person who kissed them was a Prince.

Because, in Real Life, when people are really *deep* asleep, you have to shake them, and shout, **"WAKE UP!"** in their ear, and hit them on the head with the xylophone sticks. Otherwise they don't wake up at all.

My Dad doesn't, anyway. And nor does my little brother, Tom. He falls asleep on the floor, and he doesn't wake up when Mom carries him upstairs and puts him in his pajamas and stands him up at the toilet. Not even once when he peed on his feet.

Tom is five. He's four years younger than me. I'm nine. My name is Anna.

Also, in Real Life, people don't let down their hair from towers for other people to climb up and rescue them and things, like happens in *Rapunzel*. Because you can't really climb up *hair* very well, especially not when it's still growing on someone's head. You can't climb up Emma Hendry's hair, anyway, because Graham Roberts once tried to, in PE, when Emma was up the wall bars. And Emma fell off, and Mrs. Peters wasn't pleased. And neither was Emma. She was winded. Emma's got the longest hair in school. She can sit on it if she wants to. It's never been cut. Mrs. Peters sent a note home to Emma's Mom because Emma's hair kept getting caught in doors, and drawers, and things like that, and she said, "Emma Hendry, that hair is a Death Trap!"

3

Which is true. Especially with Graham Roberts around. So now Emma's hair gets tied up, and on PE days it has to go under a net.

Anyway, this story isn't a Made-Up Story, or a Fairy Story like *Sleeping Beauty* or *Rapunzel* or anything like that. It's a Real Rescue Story. And that means that everything in it Actually Happened. I know it did, because I was there. And so was my little brother, Tom. And so was my friend Suzanne Barry, who lives next door.

This is what it says in my dictionary about what a rescue is . . .

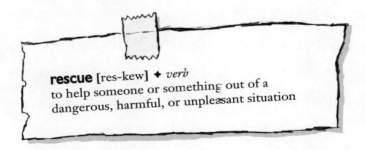

rescue [res-kew] ✦ *verb*
to help someone or something out of a dangerous, harmful, or unpleasant situation

And this is what it says in my friend Suzanne's dictionary . . .

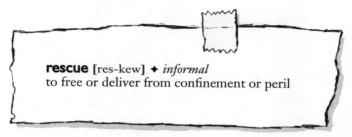

rescue [res-kew] ✦ *informal*
to free or deliver from confinement or peril

Mom said that me and Suzanne and Tom were wrong about Joe-down-the-street and that he was never even *in* any danger or peril in the first place.

She said, "Anna, Joe has gone to live with his Dad because he *wants* to. He definitely does *not* need to be rescued!"

But moms don't always know everything about who might need rescuing. Because once, when I was in Big Trouble for falling through the shed roof in the back lane by mistake, I decided that I didn't like living at

our house anymore, and I told Mom, "I wish I lived with Mrs. Rotherham up the road!"

And Mom said, "So do I!"

So I packed my bag, and I went off up the road.

When I got to Mrs. Rotherham's house, I decided I didn't *really* want to live there. But I had to by then, because that's what I'd said. So I went in. And I sat in the window by myself and stared out and didn't speak. And, after ages, there was a knock on the door. It was Tom, in his Batman pajamas and his Bob the Builder hard hat.

And Mrs. Rotherham said, "Hello, Tom. Are you all on your own?"

And Tom said, "I am Batman and Bob the Builder. I want Anna to come home."

So I did. And that was a rescue, really, what Tom

did. Because, even though I like Mrs. Rotherham a lot, I didn't *really* want to live with her. Because I'd rather live in my own house, with Tom. And Mom and Dad. And Andy and Joanne. (That's my other brother and my sister. They aren't in this story because they're older than me and Tom, and they don't really care about rabbits, or rescues.) Anyway, if Tom *hadn't* rescued me, I would probably still be living with Mrs. Rotherham now. So I'm glad he did. Because, for one thing, Mrs. Rotherham's house is at the wrong end of the road. And, for another thing, it smells a bit strange, of old things, and mothballs, like Nana's house used to. And, for an even other thing, if I lived with Mrs. Rotherham, I wouldn't live next door to Suzanne anymore.

● CHAPTER 2 ●
Anna to Suzanne

Me and Suzanne, who lives next door, have
got walkie-talkies. I talk to Suzanne on my
walkie-talkie in my house. And she talks to
me on her walkie-talkie in her house.

I hold down the button on the side and
say, "Anna to Suzanne. Anna to Suzanne.
Come in, Suzanne. Over."

And then I let go of the button, and the walkie-talkie crackles, and Suzanne says, "Suzanne to Anna. Suzanne to Anna. Receiving you loud and clear. Over."

And that's the way you're supposed to say things when you're on the walkie-talkies. Because Suzanne knows all about it from her Uncle in the army. Me and Suzanne talk on our walkie-talkies all the time, wherever we are (except in the bath, because Mom says if it falls in I'll get electrocuted to death like Ken Barlow's first wife on *Coronation Street*).

Mom says she doesn't see why me and Suzanne need walkie-talkies in our houses at all, because the wall between our house and the Barrys' house is so thin we could just put a glass to the wall and talk to each other through that. Which is true. But putting a glass to the wall isn't as good as talking

on walkie-talkies because me and Suzanne tried it.

For one thing, you both have to be in the exact same place on each side of the wall. And for another thing, you can't say anything secret because you have to say everything loud and clear or the other person can't hear it.

And, for an even other thing, if you've got squishy wallpaper on your walls, like Suzanne has in her house, the glass presses a circle shape in the wallpaper. And when Suzanne's Dad sees that, he says, **"GET IN HERE, SUZANNE! WHAT ON *EARTH* ARE THESE CIRCLE SHAPES ALL OVER THE PLACE?"**

You don't need a glass, or a walkie-talkie, or *anything* to hear Suzanne's *Dad* through the wall. You can hear everything he says, because Suzanne's Dad always shouts.

Before me and Suzanne got the walkie-talkies, we used to have a thing called the Knocking Code. This is how it worked:

I would knock three times on my bedroom wall, and if the coast was clear, Suzanne would knock back three times on her bedroom wall. And then we would both go to our windows, and open them, and crawl out, and sit outside on our window ledges, and talk about things. Like the road, and the roofs, and whether or not you go blind if you stare straight at the sun.

The only thing with the Knocking Code was, sometimes, if there were other noises going on, Suzanne couldn't hear my knocks. And then I had to crawl out onto my window ledge, and over to Suzanne's, to look in through her window, to see if I could see her. And one time when I did that, when Suzanne wasn't there, my window closed behind me. By itself. And I couldn't get it open again. I banged on my window. And nobody came. And I banged on Suzanne's window. And nobody came. And it started raining. And I sat on the window ledge. And I got very wet. And I shouted, **"HELLO!"** and **"HELP!"** and **"I'M ON THE WINDOW LEDGE!"** And after a while I wondered what would be worse, staying on the window ledge and catching my death of cold, like Nana always used to say I would, or jumping off the window ledge and breaking both my legs.

And just when I was wondering that, Mr. Tucker, who lives opposite, came out of his house to put his trash cans out.

So I shouted down, **"HELP! Mr. TUCKER! UP HERE! I'M ON THE WINDOW LEDGE!"**

Mr. Tucker's got a lot of medals from the War. For flying planes, and fighting, and

blowing things up and all that. He doesn't fly planes anymore, though. He's too old. Most of the time what Mr. Tucker does is go up and down the road picking up litter. Nana used to say Mr. Tucker was "waging a one-man war against rubbish."

Mr. Tucker put his trash cans down, and he said, "HALLO, LOOK KEEN, WHAT'S THIS?"

I said, **"IT'S ME!"**

"AHA, POPSIE. ON A PROTEST UP THERE, ARE YOU?"

I don't like being called Popsie. Sometimes when Mr. Tucker calls me it, I pretend I can't hear him. But I didn't do that this time because of being stuck out on the window ledge in the dark and the rain and everything, and needing to get rescued.

So I said, **"NO, I'M NOT ON A PROTEST."** Because I wasn't. **"I'M STUCK."**

"STUCK, IS IT?"

"YES," I said. **"I CAME OUT, AND NOW I CAN'T GET BACK IN."**

Mr. Tucker said, "NOT BINDING ON?"

And I said, **"WHAT?"**

Because sometimes it's hard to know what Mr. Tucker means, with him having been in the War and everything.

"COMPLAINING ABOUT THE CONDITIONS?"

"NO," I said. **"I CAME OUT TO SEE SUZANNE, AND THE WINDOW CLOSED BEHIND ME."**

"AHA, BOTCHED OP, EH? SIT TIGHT. I'LL GET ME KIT."

And he went and got his long ladder, and he put it up to the window and held it steady at the bottom, and said, "THAT'S   I T . YOU'VE   GOT   THE   GREEN. CHOCKS AWAY."

And I climbed down.

I stood behind Mr. Tucker, and Mr. Tucker rang our doorbell.

Mom   opened   the   door. And Tom was with her, in his Batman pajamas, and he was pleased to see Mr. Tucker, because talking to Mr. Tucker is one of Tom's favorite things.

Tom gave Mr. Tucker the salute. And Mr. Tucker gave Tom the salute back. Because that's what Tom and Mr. Tucker always do when they see each other.

And Mr. Tucker said, "You're in your best blues there, Old Chum. Bang on target, those jimjams. Batman, eh? Smashing, Basher."

And Tom stuck his chest out.

And Mr. Tucker said to Mom, "Missing one of your mob, Mrs. Morris? Found this one trying to bail out."

And he pointed behind him. I poked my head round.

Mom said, "Anna, what are you doing? Why are you wet?"

We went inside, and I told Mom about what had happened with the Knocking Code, and how I went out the window, and climbed over to Suzanne's, and how my window closed behind me, and how I couldn't get back in, and how the rain came down, and how I banged on the windows, and shouted for help, and how I climbed all the way down the long ladder by myself.

Mom didn't look very happy. And I thought I was going to be in Big Trouble again, because she said "*Anna . . .*" the way she always does.

But Mr. Tucker butted in. "What a line!" he said. "No, no, no. *Here's* how it went. I *smell* something's up, you see—instinct. Go out on me own, no Second Dickey. Clock Popsie, dead ahead, ten angels up and about to bail. Say to myself, 'Look lively, Wing Commander. Your twelve o'clock, young blond job doing the dutch!' I get weaving right away. Caught some bad flack off Mrs. Tucker, '*RAYMOND!*' and all that. Corkscrew out of it. Ladder up. Popsie down. Safe and sound. Spot on. (Be surprised if I don't get a gong as it goes.) No need to debrief Blondie, though, Chiefy. Caught a packet on her way down, lot of offensive fire. Tore a strip off her myself, of course. Badly botched op, and the clot hadn't packed her chute correctly. All in order now, though. No harm done. Prob'ly do with a brew up."

Mom looked at me. I was cold. And I was dripping quite a lot on the carpet. And she started smiling. And Mr. Tucker started smiling too. And then Mom and Mr. Tucker started laughing. And they got The Hysterics, which is what you get when you start laughing and then you can't stop.

But I didn't get The Hysterics. Because

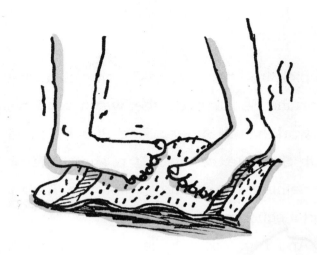

my feet were going blue, and anyway, like Tom said, "It's not that funny."

Mom got me a towel and made some tea.

And Mr. Tucker drank his and said, "Better get on, or I'll catch another packet off Mrs. Tucker. If you fancy pulling your finger out tomorrow, I shall be out plugging away at this litter situation again. Four Coke cans, three grocery bags, and a half-eaten carton of chicken chow mein today. Doesn't do, Popsie, doesn't do. O-eight-hundred hours, eh?"

Normally, I tell Mr. Tucker I'm too busy

to pick up litter. Especially on a Saturday morning. Because I'd rather watch cartoons, or work on the Super-Speed-Bike-Machine with Suzanne, or sit on the shed roof or something. But seeing as how Mr. Tucker had rescued me, I said, "Okay."

And Tom said that he was coming too, because he loves doing things with Mr. Tucker. Especially picking up litter. He follows him up and down and holds the trash bag open for Mr. Tucker to put the rubbish in.

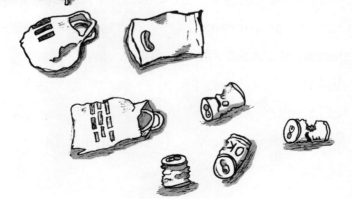

Mr. Tucker said, "Spot on, Tom." And he messed up

Tom's hair. And Tom and Mr. Tucker gave each other the salute again. And then Mr. Tucker went home.

Mr. Tucker isn't like the people who do rescues in Made-Up Stories or Fairy Tales or anything like that. Because no one ever makes Sleeping Beauty or Rapunzel go on a litter pick.

Anyway, after that I didn't go out on the window ledge again.

The next day, me and Suzanne told Mrs. Rotherham all about what happened with Mr. Tucker, and the Knocking Code, and how we couldn't go out of our windows to talk anymore. Mrs. Rotherham got us some ice cream, and she said, "Mmm, let me think. . . ." And then she winked. "I've got just the things for you two if I can lay my hands on them."

And she went into one of her cupboards. And she found two walkie-talkies. Not toy walkie-talkies like some people have. Real walkie-talkies that Mrs. Rotherham used to use when she was in the police about a million years ago.

Mrs. Rotherham cleaned the walkie-talkies up, and got them working, and she gave them to us to keep.

If anything ever happens to my Mom and Dad, I'll probably go and live with Mrs. Rotherham, as long as she doesn't mind

Tom coming too, even though she's old, and her house smells a bit strange. Because she's got lots of good stuff in her cupboards, and she always gives you ice cream, and she never tells you not to do things.

❝ CHAPTER 3 ❞
The Old Rabbit and the New Cat

Before everything happened with Joe-
down-the-street, before he went away and
had to get rescued, I didn't really mind all
that much whether he was down the road
or not. Because most of the time, when he
was down the road, Joe just did things on his
own. And partly that was because Joe didn't
want to do the things me and Suzanne were
doing. And partly that was because me and
Suzanne didn't want to do the things Joe
was doing. But mainly it was because Joe

wouldn't come out of his garden because he had to guard his New Rabbit.

Most people who've got rabbits don't really guard them all that much. Because they probably think that when a rabbit's in its hutch, nothing bad can happen to it. But Joe-down-the-street knows that even in their hutches, rabbits aren't always safe. Because Joe used to have another rabbit, called the *Old* Rabbit, that he got from his Dad, when his Dad still lived at Joe's house, before he went away.

And once, when Joe was playing out the back with me and Suzanne, a cat went in Joe's garden, and looked in at Joe's Old Rabbit, sitting in its hutch. And the Old Rabbit was so scared when it saw the cat that it panicked and died. And that's why, when Joe's Mom got him a New Rabbit, Joe started guarding it straightaway.

Joe's Mom's Boyfriend said, "The Old Rabbit was daft to die just because a cat *looked* at it." Because "It's not like the cat could open the hutch."

But the Old Rabbit *wasn't* daft really, because, like Suzanne said, "You don't have

26

time to think about things like that when you're about to die of fright."

And it isn't just rabbits that can die of fright either. Anyone can. Suzanne knows all about it, after she saw a show on TV called *Scared to Death*.

And she said, "A man died of fright when his wife jumped out on him from inside the wardrobe."

Which the wife said was meant to be a joke. But like Tom said, "It wasn't a very funny one."

Suzanne always gets to watch all the good stuff on TV. Not like me and Tom. My Mom changes the channel and puts *Coronation Street* on instead. When Suzanne told Joe all about the *Scared to Death* show, and the man who died of fright, Joe said he was going to jump out on his Mom's Boyfriend from their wardrobe and see if it worked.

But he never got the chance because Joe's Mom's Boyfriend stopped being her Boyfriend soon after that. And he started being Joe's Babysitter's Boyfriend instead. And Joe never saw him again.

Joe's got a different babysitter now, called Brian.

Anyway, the thing with Joe's Old Rabbit was, it wasn't just *any* old cat that scared it to death. In fact it wasn't an *old* cat at all. It was a *new* cat. *Our* New Cat, which is a wild cat that we got off a farm. And everyone is scared of it: me, and Mom, and even the Milkman. Because the New Cat is a *mad* cat. And it attacks anything it can. The only one who isn't afraid of the New Cat is Tom.

This is a list me and Suzanne made of all the things that the New Cat has killed . . .

ANNA'S AND SUZANNE'S LIST OF THINGS THAT THE NEW CAT HAS KILLED

6 mice

2 frogs (One might have been a toad. After the New Cat got it, it was hard to tell.)

4 blackbirds

2 jackdaws

1 rat

12 spiders

4 moths

1 shrew

3 bees (the New Cat doesn't even mind when it gets stung)

Whenever the New Cat kills something, me and Suzanne do a funeral for it. We put the body in a box, and we bury it in the back lane. We've buried so many things in our bit of the back lane that we've run out of room. So now we have to bury things in Miss Matheson's bit too. Miss Matheson lives next door, on the other side. Our house is between hers and Suzanne's.

Miss Matheson doesn't like it when she sees me and Suzanne burying things in her bit of the back lane.

She shouts, **"YOU GIRLS GET OUT OF IT! THAT'S MY GARDEN, NOT A GRAVEYARD. GET AWAY FROM MY GLADIOLI!"**

And she phones Mom to complain.

I think we should be allowed to bury whatever we want in Miss Matheson's bit of the back lane. Because Miss Matheson ran over our Old Cat, which never used to kill anything, and if she hadn't done that, we would never have got the New Cat in the first place. And then it wouldn't be here to keep killing things all the time.

❝ CHAPTER 4 ❞
You Be the Dog

Joe guards the New Rabbit with a Super Soaker water pistol. Sometimes he marches up and down in front of the hutch with his Super Soaker. And sometimes he stands still by the hutch with his Super Soaker. And sometimes he sits on the hutch with his Super Soaker. And if anything comes anywhere near Joe's garden, like a cat, or

a pigeon, or an ant, Joe blasts it and shouts, "TAKE THAT! AND DON'T EVER COME BACK!"

Before Joe started guarding his rabbit all the time, me and Suzanne and Joe used to do lots of things together, like going on the rope swing at the top of the road, and sliding down the stairs in sleeping bags, and seeing who could hold their breath the longest before they die. And sometimes we played games that everyone knows, like Shops, and Schools, and Prisons, and things. And sometimes we played our own made-up games, like Dingo the Dog, and Mountain Rescue, and breaking the world record on the Super-Speed-Bike-Machine.

Here's what happens in Dingo the Dog. There's a school, for dogs, and Suzanne is the teacher. (Suzanne knows all about dog schools because she used to take her dog

Barney to one, before her Dad said he was allergic and sent Barney to live on a farm.) Anyway, Suzanne tells all the dogs what to do, like "Stay," and "Roll over," and "Heel," and all that. (There aren't real dogs in the class. We just pretend. There's only one real dog on our road, and it belongs to Miss Matheson. It's the same size as a guinea pig, and we aren't allowed to play with it.)

Anyway, there are lots of pretend dogs in the class, and they're all doing what they are told. And I come to the class with my dog, which is a bad dog called Dingo. (It's really Joe-down-the-street, on his hands and knees, with Barney's old collar on and a leash.) And Dingo goes around sniffing all the other dogs, and Suzanne tells him off. And then Dingo spots a dog he really hates, and he barks, and goes crazy, and slips his collar off, and chases the dog around the

room, and right out of the class. And I run up and down the road shouting, **"Dingo, Dingo, here, boy!"** and try to get him back. But Dingo hides in the bushes, and howls, and tears up the flower beds, and pees on trees and everything. And all the other dogs in the class go mad and start chasing each other too. And their owners complain, and ask Suzanne for their money back.

It's a pretty good game.

But it's no good without Joe, because no one else can do Dingo. Because Suzanne is only good at telling the dogs what to do. And I'm only good at doing the chasing. And once Tom tried to be Dingo, but he didn't like the leash, and he wasn't any good at being bad. Because he just sat when Suzanne told him to sit, and stayed when she told him to stay. And then, when Suzanne told him he was supposed to be a *bad* dog, he bit her. On the arm. Really hard. And Suzanne screamed. And went home. And Tom had to go in the house and sit with Mom and have a cookie.

And Mom took Tom off the leash, and said, "Best not to play Dingo the Dog anymore, Anna."

Another game we used to play with Joe-down-the-street is the Mountain Rescue Game. We play it inside when it's really raining and we aren't allowed out. We don't play it in Suzanne's house, though, not since her Dad tripped over the rescue rope and went flying down the stairs, and said, **"THIS IS A STAIRCASE, SUZANNE, NOT SNOWDONIA! YOU CHILDREN COULD'VE KILLED ME!"**

Anyway, what happens in Mountain Rescue is, Suzanne goes to the top of the stairs, which is the top of the mountain,

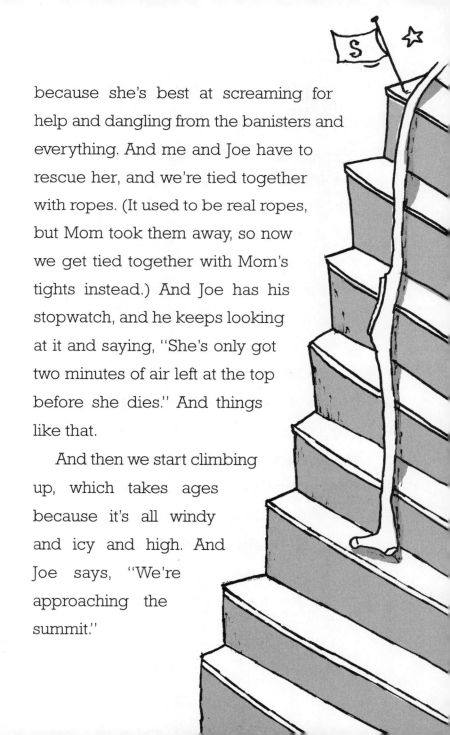

because she's best at screaming for help and dangling from the banisters and everything. And me and Joe have to rescue her, and we're tied together with ropes. (It used to be real ropes, but Mom took them away, so now we get tied together with Mom's tights instead.) And Joe has his stopwatch, and he keeps looking at it and saying, "She's only got two minutes of air left at the top before she dies." And things like that.

And then we start climbing up, which takes ages because it's all windy and icy and high. And Joe says, "We're approaching the summit."

And then he says, *"AVALANCHE!"*

And that's when we fall all the way down. And land at the bottom. And then we have to climb all the way back up again. In the end we bring Suzanne down on a stretcher, which is a sleeping bag. And sometimes she's alive, and other times she's dead. We don't do the Mountain Rescue Game anymore, though, because Joe's the only one with a stopwatch, and last time, when me and Suzanne played Mountain Rescue on our own, when I got to the top, we argued about whether Suzanne was dead or not. Because Suzanne said she was, even though she wasn't. And she wouldn't help me get her down the mountain. And that's why the stretcher slipped and Suzanne went all the way down on her own, and landed on her head. And then she went home.

And Mom said, "Best not to play Mountain Rescue anymore, Anna."

And we aren't allowed on the Super-Speed-Bike-Machine anymore either. The Super-Speed-Bike-Machine is my bike, with Joe's stunt pegs on the back wheel for standing on, and Tom's old training wheels on the sides, and Suzanne's trailer tied on behind. Before Joe's Dad stopped living at Joe's house, me and Suzanne and Joe-down-the-street used to work on the Super-Speed-Bike-Machine all the time, cleaning it, and putting spokies on the wheels, and streamers on the handlebars, and stickers on the crossbar, and painting the trailer, and pumping up the tires, and repairing the punctures, and all that. And after we worked on it, we would take it right up to the top of the back lane, by Miss Matheson's garden, which used to drive her dog mad, and

streamers

spokies

Trailer

Stickers

Training wheels and stunt pegs

Miss Matheson would run out and shout, "YOU KIDS GET THAT CONTRAPTION AWAY FROM MY GATE!"

And then I would get on the seat, and Suzanne would sit on the handlebars, and Joe would stand on the stunt pegs, and Tom would kneel in the trailer, and Joe's Dad would stand at the bottom of the back lane. And we'd all say, **"THREE, TWO, ONE, BLAST OFF!"**

And then Joe pushed off from the stunt

pegs, and Suzanne leaned back, and Tom held tight to the trailer, and I pedaled my fastest, and we all went flying down the back lane, over the hump, right to the bottom, where Joe put his foot out to slow the Super-Speed-Bike-Machine down, and Joe's Dad grabbed hold to stop us from going into the road. And then we checked the seconds on the stopwatch, and if it was a world record, we put it in the record book. And if it wasn't, we went all the way back up to the top and did it again. And sometimes we did it all day.

Once, after Joe's Dad stopped living at Joe's house, and Joe's Old Rabbit died, and Joe started guarding his New Rabbit all the time, me and Suzanne and Tom went on the Super-Speed-Bike-Machine on our own. But Joe wasn't there to put his foot out at the end to slow us down, and his Dad wasn't there to grab the Super-Speed-Bike-Machine and stop it from going in the road, and it did go in the road, and it only stopped when it hit the curb on the other side, and then Tom flew out of the trailer, and the Super-Speed-Bike-Machine went over on its side, and a van had to screech to a stop. And Tom had to go to the hospital and get six sticky stitches in his head.

And Mom said, "Best not to go on the Super-Speed-Bike-Machine again, Anna."

And she put it at the back of the shed, under an old sheet, behind the stepladders, and the plant stakes, and the broken old floorboards.

Anyway, when Joe first started guarding the New Rabbit, me and Suzanne sometimes used to go and guard it with him. Joe told us all the rules, and we took our Super Soakers and we marched up and down and blasted anything that moved. But after a while, especially when nothing much came except squirrels and starlings and daddy longlegs and things, me and Suzanne got sick of guarding the New Rabbit.

And we said, "Let's go and do something else, like make plans, or do Dizzy Ducklings, or sit on the shed roof instead."

But Joe always said, "No."

And one day, when Tom came to guard the New Rabbit with us, Joe said that Tom wasn't allowed in his garden because of him liking the New Cat. And he blasted Tom with the Super Soaker and said, **"Take that! And don't ever come back!"**

And Tom fell over. And he ran up the

road. And me and Joe argued after that. And Joe's Mom sent me home. And I got in Big Trouble. Even though it was Joe's fault in the first place, because, like I said, "It's not Tom's fault that the New Cat is his friend!"

But Mom said she didn't care, because, "Whatever happens, Anna, you don't beat people about the head with Super Soakers."

And after that I didn't go and see Joe-down-the-street and guard the New Rabbit much anymore. Apart from when Mom made me. Because I'd rather do other things. Like going on the walkie-talkies, or doing funerals, or finding wood lice. And, anyway, me and Suzanne had our clubs to do, which no one else was allowed in.

44

ANNA'S AND SUZANNE'S CLUBS THAT NO ONE ELSE (EXCEPT SOMETIMES TOM) IS ALLOWED IN

1. Shed Club

Make up a password

Don't let anyone in who doesn't know the
   password (except Tom when he forgets it)

Make plans

Don't tell anyone the plans

2. Worm Club

Collect worms

Put the worms in the worm box in the shed

Write down how many worms there are in the
   record book (most number of worms in a
   day so far = 43)

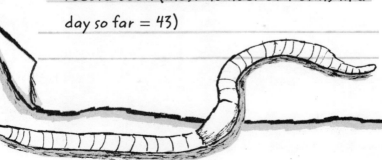

3. Bug Club

Same as Worm Club but with bugs instead of worms

Cover the bugs with a lid or they get away

Put holes in the lid or they die

4. Spy Club

Spy on people with the binoculars Mrs. Rotherham
    gave us

Write what people are up to in the notepad

People we have got pages on in the notepad are . . .

1. Miss Matheson

2. The Lollipop Lady

3. Mr. Tucker

4. Suzanne's Dad

5. Joe's Mom

6. Joe's Mom's Old
    Boyfriend

7. Joe's Old Babysitter

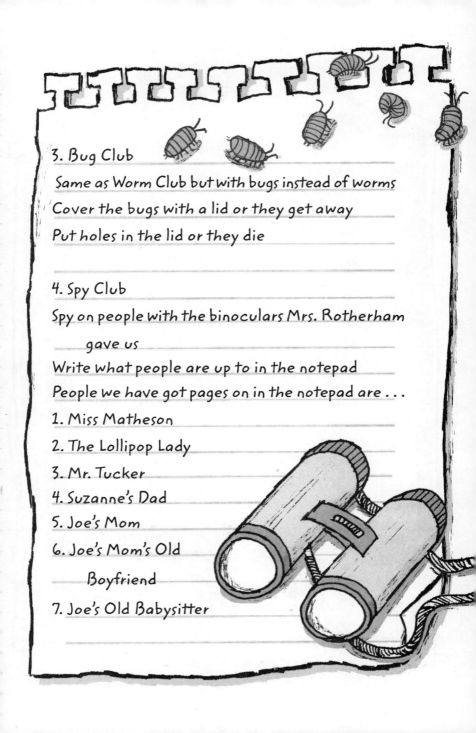

Me and Suzanne aren't supposed to do Spy Club anymore because last time Miss Matheson saw us looking in at her through her window, and she phoned Mom to complain.

And Mom said, "It's rude to spy on people and write down what they're doing, Anna. Especially when they're in the bathroom."

And she said if she found out that we were doing Spy Club again, we would be in Big Trouble.

So we put the binoculars and the notepad away, at the back of the shed, on the shelf above the broken floorboards and the stepladders and the Super-Speed-Bike-Machine.

Sometimes Tom does clubs with me and Suzanne, except Worm Club, because he says worms wriggle his skin, but most of the time he forgets he's meant to be looking for weevils and wood lice and things, and goes to see Mom and get a cookie, or to talk to Mr. Tucker about his old sports car instead. Doing clubs is pretty good, and so is sitting on the shed roof, and going on the walkie-talkies and things, but not as good as before, when Joe didn't have to guard his rabbit, and Joe's Dad was still on the road, and we did Dingo the Dog, and Mountain Rescue, and going on the Super-Speed-Bike-Machine.

49

✤ CHAPTER 5 ✤
A Rabbit Pie Chart

Joe couldn't guard his New Rabbit *all* the time though, because, like his Mom said, "Sometimes you have to do other things, Joe, like sleep, and eat, and go to school."

But whenever he *wasn't* doing those sorts of things, Joe stayed in his garden, because he said, "The less time the New Rabbit gets guarded, the more chance there is of the New Rabbit getting got."

Which is probably true.

But some people didn't think Joe needed

to guard his New Rabbit at all. Mrs. Peters told Joe that she didn't think so, the day we made pie chart mobiles at school.

That morning Mrs. Peters said, "Right, everyone. Here is a math problem. There are twenty-four hours in a day. If Janet spends ten hours in bed, and six hours at school, how many hours has Janet got left for doing other things?"

And she wrote it on the whiteboard. Some people put their hands up, like Emma Hendry, but not Joe, because even though Joe is good at math, he isn't very good at putting his hand up. Which is different from Emma Hendry. Because Emma Hendry is good at putting her hand up, but she isn't very good at math.

Anyway, even though Joe didn't put his hand up, Mrs. Peters said, "Joe, why don't you have a go?"

And Joe said, "Twenty-four hours minus ten hours sleeping equals fourteen hours; and fourteen hours minus six hours at school equals eight hours, so Janet's got eight hours left to do what she wants."

And he said it really fast. Just like that. And he was right, because Mrs. Peters said, "Very good. Well done, Joe."

And she wrote it on the board like this:

$$24-10=14$$
$$14-6=8$$

I didn't get that answer. I didn't get any answer, because for one thing, I'm even worse at math than Emma Hendry is, especially if I have to do it in my head. And for another thing, Mrs. Peters had said here is *a* math problem and that was actually *two* problems. And for an even other thing, Graham Roberts, who sits next to me, drew a picture in his book of a girl called Janet.

And he drew some fumes coming off Janet's bum, and he wrote, **Janet has eight hours a day to drop bum bombs.** And I got The Hysterics. And Mrs. Peters said I had to go and stand outside the classroom and do deep breathing until I calmed down.

When I came back, Mrs. Peters drew a big circle on the whiteboard, and she said that the circle was "a day." And she drew twenty-four slices in the circle, which was "one for each hour." And she colored some of the slices in to show the different things Janet did in a day. And she said it was called a "pie chart."

This is what Mrs. Peters's pie chart of Janet's day looked like:

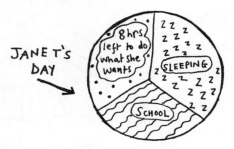

In the afternoon Mrs. Peters helped us all do our own pie charts. And we could put anything we liked in them. Mine was like this:

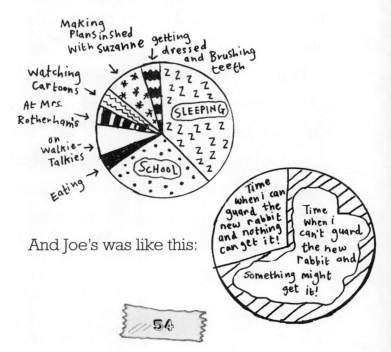

And Joe's was like this:

Later on we colored our pie charts in. Mrs. Peters said our pie charts were so good, she was going to cut them out and put a string through each one and hang them from the ceiling to make mobiles. Emma Hendry asked Mrs. Peters why pie charts are called pie charts. And Mrs. Peters said it's because they look like pies. Which is true. They don't taste like pies, though, because Graham Roberts licked his. And he got blue felt-tip all over his tongue. And I got The Hysterics again. And Mrs. Peters sent me back out of the classroom. And Graham Roberts had to put his tongue under the tap.

When the bell rang, Mrs. Peters said she wanted to talk to Joe about his pie chart and some other work he'd done, like his poem about the rabbit that dies when it gets dark, and his story about the rabbit that can't get to sleep, and his painting of the rabbit being guarded with guns. Me and Suzanne stayed behind to wait for Joe, to walk home. Mrs. Peters told Joe he wasn't in trouble. She said she just wondered whether he might be worried about something. Like his rabbit, maybe.

Joe told Mrs. Peters that he wasn't worried. And Mrs. Peters asked if he was sure.

And Joe said, "Yes."

And Mrs. Peters said that that was good. Because she didn't think that Joe needed to worry about his rabbit. Because she thought his rabbit was very safe.

"Because," she said, "rabbits are pretty tough, you know, Joe."

And Joe said, "I know."

Even though he didn't really think so.

Mrs. Peters asked me and Suzanne what we thought.

And I said, "*Some* rabbits are tough."

And Suzanne said, "Joe's Old Rabbit wasn't. It got scared to death by Anna's Cat."

"Did it?" said Mrs. Peters.

And Suzanne said, "Yes."

And Mrs. Peters asked, "How?"

And Suzanne told her, "In its hutch."

"Oh. I see. That's not very nice, is it?"

And Suzanne said, "No."

Because it wasn't. Especially not for Joe. Or the Old Rabbit.

Mrs. Peters asked, "Do you want to tell me about your Old Rabbit, Joe?"

And Joe said, "No."

And Mrs. Peters said, "Okay."

And then she said that she thought that what had happened to Joe's Old Rabbit was "very sad and very bad luck." But she didn't think that it meant that something bad was going to happen to Joe's *New* Rabbit. Because she thought that it was "a one-off." Which is when something only happens once. And then she said, "Lightning doesn't strike twice, as they say."

Joe didn't say anything.

Mrs. Peters said, "What do you think, Joe?"

And Joe said, "Okay."

And Mrs. Peters smiled at Joe and said, "Okay, then." And she gave him a stroke on the head, which Mrs. Peters doesn't normally do. And then she said, "Have a good weekend." Because it was Friday. And me and Suzanne and Joe walked home.

On the way, I asked Joe if he was going to stop guarding his New Rabbit now.

And Joe said, "No. Mrs. Peters is wrong about lightning not striking twice, because there was a man in America called Roy Sullivan who got struck by lightning seven times."

And that's true, because I looked on the computer when I got home, and before he died, Roy Sullivan was always getting struck by lightning. And his wife got struck by lightning too. So if anyone ever says that lightning doesn't strike twice, they're wrong. Because sometimes it does. And sometimes it strikes seven times, like it did with Roy Sullivan. And that's why they called him "The Human Lightbulb."

I told Suzanne what it said on the computer about people getting struck by lightning millions of times and everything. And about Roy Sullivan. And how he was the human lightbulb and all that. And I said, "Want to see?"

And Suzanne said, "No."

And I said, "Oh."

And Suzanne said, "I already know."

Suzanne always says she already knows when you try to tell her things.

I said, "Well, Roy Sullivan and his wife aren't the only ones, because there are lots of people who've got struck by lightning twice, like his wife, and lots of trees too."

And Suzanne said, "I know" again.

And I said, "No, you don't."

Because she didn't.

And Suzanne said she did know actually, and even if she *didn't* know, she didn't care. Because what she *really* didn't know was why everyone kept going on about lightning all the time. Like me, and Joe, and Mrs. Peters.

Because, she said, "Lightning hasn't even got anything to do with it, because it isn't lightning that Joe is guarding the New Rabbit from. It's other things, like cats!"

I said I wouldn't show Suzanne anything on the computer ever again. Or tell her any more things about anything. Especially not Roy Sullivan. Not even if she asked.

✎ CHAPTER 6 ✎
Joe-Down-the-Street's Dad's Van

Sometimes me and Suzanne go down to
the bottom of the back lane, and we take
the walkie-talkies, and we stand back-to-
back. And Suzanne walks *down* the road,
and I walk *up* the road, because we
want to know how far apart we can
go before the walkie-talkies stop
working. When we've gone twenty

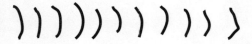

steps apart, we stop, and Suzanne says, "Suzanne to Anna. Suzanne to Anna. Come in, Anna. What's your position? Over."

And I say, "Anna to Suzanne. Anna to Suzanne. I'm at the chestnut tree. Over."

And then Suzanne says, "Copy that. Chestnut tree. Are you receiving me? Over."

And I say, "Yes. Over."

And then Suzanne says, "You're supposed to say, 'Receiving you loud and clear. Over.'"

And I say, "Oh. Receiving you loud and clear. Over."

And Suzanne says, "Copy that. Over and out."

And then we walk twenty more steps apart, and say the same stuff

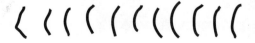

again, about where we are, and whether we can hear each other and everything. Only I don't always do all the "Come ins," and the "Copies," and the "Over and outs" and all that, even though Suzanne says her Uncle in the army said you should. Because sometimes I forget. And sometimes it takes too long. And sometimes I'd rather say something else instead.

Once, when me and Suzanne were seeing how far apart we could go, I got all the way down to the Bottom Bus Stop, and Suzanne got all the way up to the Police Station. Which are *ages* apart from each other, at opposite ends of the village, and the walkie-talkies still worked. But that's as far apart as we've got, because

Suzanne's not allowed past the Police Station, or the Bottom Bus Stop, because her Dad says it's **"OUT OF BOUNDS!"**

I don't know if I'm allowed past the Police Station or the Bottom Bus Stop or not. My Dad has never said anything about bounds to me before. I probably am, though. I'm normally allowed to do more things than Suzanne.

Because even though Suzanne's Mom doesn't mind Suzanne doing most things, like going out of the back lane, or not taking a coat, or doing relay races up the road in bare feet, Suzanne's Dad minds Suzanne doing a *lot* of things. And if it was only up to him, Suzanne probably wouldn't be allowed to do anything at all. Except eat her dinner, and brush her teeth, and go to bed, and things like that. Suzanne's Dad is different from my Dad. If you ask my Dad if you can do something, he says, "You can play on the highway as far as I'm concerned, Anna. But you'd better ask your Mom."

But Suzanne's Dad just says, **"NO!"**

And he's not the sort of Dad you can say, **"Ahhhh, but whyyYYYyy, though, Dad? PleeEEase?"** to. Because he won't change his mind. He'll only say, **"RIGHT, THAT'S IT. ROOM!"**

Anyway, this time we didn't get anywhere near the Bottom Bus Stop and the Police Station because we were just standing back-to-back at the bottom of our road, ready to go, when we saw Joe's Dad's van coming.

We knew it was Joe's Dad's van because it said BARRY WALKER: SMALL BUILDING WORKS, RENOVATION, AND REFURBISHMENT on the side.

The van stopped right outside Joe's

house, where it always used to stop when Joe's Dad still lived there. So me and Suzanne stopped doing the walkie-talkie testing and decided to do some spying instead. Because, even though we aren't supposed to do Spy Club anymore because Mom says we're banned, sometimes we *have* to do it if it's really important.

Suzanne ran up the road and got the binoculars, and the notepad, and we turned the walkie-talkies off and crouched down low behind a car at the bottom of the road. Suzanne looked round from behind the car through the binoculars.

"What can you see?" I said.

"Joe's Dad's hair."

Suzanne passed the binoculars to me.

She was right. You *could* see Joe's Dad's hair. And you couldn't see much else. Because for one thing we were too close to Joe's Dad to really need the binoculars. Because the whole point of binoculars is that they are for looking at things that are far away. And for another thing, Joe's Dad has got a lot of hair. It's long and brown and curly.

"He's got split ends," Suzanne said. "And he's going gray." She wrote in the notepad: Saturday, 9:45 a.m. Joe's Dad outside Joe's house in his van.

And then she put: Split ends. Going gray.

Suzanne knows all about hair because her Mom is a hairdresser.

Suzanne's Mom cut Joe's Dad's hair when he still lived on our road. When Joe's Dad stopped living on our road, Suzanne's Mom said to my Mom, "What a shame."

And my Mom said, "I know. Such a lovely man."

And Suzanne's Mom said, "And such lovely hair."

And my Mom said, "Yeah."

And they both shook their heads for ages.

Suzanne's Mom cuts my Dad's hair too, and Suzanne's Dad's. She doesn't say *they've* got lovely hair, though. My Dad and Suzanne's Dad are mostly bald.

Anyway, Joe's Dad got out of his van, and he went round to the back of it and opened the van doors, and took out three big brown boxes, and he carried the boxes up the path to Joe's house, and he rang on Joe's doorbell and went inside.

Suzanne wrote down: 9:48 a.m. Joe's Dad takes three big brown boxes into Joe's house.

"Maybe Joe's Dad has come back to live at Joe's house," said Suzanne.

And I said I hoped he had. Because then he would fix the rope swing at the top of the road, where the rope was caught up and the tire had come off.

Joe's Dad is good at fixing things. He can fix bikes and binoculars and buildings and everything. He fixed our shed roof after I fell through it, so me and Suzanne could sit on it again.

And he's good at other things too. Like teaching you how to do relay races, and pushing you round in his wheelbarrow, and getting you with the hose when he's cleaning his van.

When Joe's Dad stopped living down the road, me and Tom asked our Dad if *he* would get us with the hose. Dad said, "Why not cut out the middle man? Stick your heads under the outside tap if you want to get wet."

"*Joe's* Dad gets

us with the hose," I said. "It's fun."

"Yeah, yeah, yeah," Dad said. "I used to be fun. And I used to have hair."

I asked Dad when his hair fell out.

Dad said, "The day you were born." And then he laughed. Even though it wasn't funny.

Tom told Dad, "Joe-down-the-street's Dad has got hair, and a van, and a cement mixer, and that's why he's the best Dad on the road."

"Right!" Dad said. And he grabbed Tom and tickled him. But not for long, because if you tickle Tom too much, he wets himself. And then he gets upset. And also because the football came on. And Dad doesn't do anything when that happens. Except drink his beer and shout at the TV, and put his hands over his eyes.

Anyway, me and Suzanne were crouching quietly behind the car at the bottom of the road, waiting to see what happened.

And then Tom came running down the road, and he saw us and he shouted, **"WHAT ARE YOU DOING?"**

"Shh," I said, "we're spying. Get down."

And Tom got down behind the car as well.

Joe's Dad came out of Joe's house, holding one of the big brown boxes. He went round to the back of the van, and he opened the doors and put the box in the van.

And Tom stood up, and he said, "Hello."

Joe's Dad looked around to see where the voice had come from.

"Tom!" I whispered. "Get down!"

But he didn't. Tom doesn't really care about spying. He cares more about other things, like Joe's Dad's van.

"Hello, lad," said Joe's Dad.

"Can I go in your van?" Tom said.

"Ah, not today, Tommy."

"Why?" Tom said.

Because that's Tom's favorite question. And because Joe's Dad always used to let him get in his van and look at all the tools, and once he let Tom put sand in the cement mixer. And that was about the best thing Tom had ever done. Except for when Mr. Tucker let Tom sit on his knee in the driver's seat of his old sports car and put his driving gloves and goggles on. And drive up and down the road, and honk the horn.

Anyway, Joe's Dad said, "Bit busy today. Next time, eh, Tom? Promise."

And Tom said, "Okay."

And they shook on it. And Joe's Dad went back into Joe's house. And Tom went

to talk to Mr. Tucker. Mr. Tucker is never too busy. Especially not for Tom.

Me and Suzanne stayed waiting. After a while Joe's Dad came out of Joe's house again with another brown box. And he went round the back of the van, and opened the doors, and put it in. And then he went back into the house, and got the last brown box and put that in the van too. He shut the van doors. And got in the van himself.

And then Joe and his Mom came out of the house. And Joe went over to his rabbit hutch, and he checked the latch, and arranged his plastic soldiers on the roof, and then he got his Super Soaker, and he pumped it up, and blasted some ants. And then he gave his Mom a cuddle. And he got in the van, in the front, next to his Dad. And he put his seat belt on. And then he took his seat belt off again, and he got out of the van. And he went over to the rabbit hutch. And checked the latch again. And rearranged his plastic soldiers.

And then Joe's Dad got out of the van too. And he talked to Joe's Mom for a bit, and he gave Joe a cuddle. And then Joe's Dad got back in the van by himself. And he drove away.

And Joe ran out of his garden, down the road after the van. And the van stopped. And Joe got in it. And the van drove off. And Joe looked out the window. Me and Suzanne waved at Joe, but Joe didn't wave back.

When Joe and Joe's Dad and the van were gone, Joe's Mom sat down on the doorstep by herself. Suzanne looked through the binoculars. And she wrote in the book: 10:45 a.m. Joe-down-the-street's Mom sits down on the step and cries.

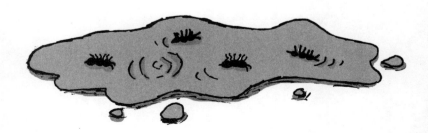

CHAPTER 7
The Tale of Peter Rabbit

Me and Suzanne told my Mom all about Joe's Dad, and his van, and Joe, and the boxes.

Mom said, "Oh, poor Pam." (Which is Joe's Mom's name.)

I asked, "Why?"

"Never mind," Mom said. "I'm popping down the road."

"What for?"

"Nothing."

"Are you going to spy?" asked Suzanne.

"No, Suzanne," Mom said, "I am not going to spy. I'm just going to see Joe's Mom."

And I said, "We'll come."

"No," Mom said, "you won't."

Suzanne asked Mom, "Why?"

"Because I want to talk to Pam on my own," Mom said. And off she went.

When Mom came back, after ages, me and Suzanne were waiting for her on the garden wall.

"Where has Joe gone?" I asked.

Mom said, "To stay with his Dad."

Me and Suzanne followed Mom into the house.

Suzanne asked, "Where's that?"

"Not far," Mom said. "At his apartment."

"In the village?" I asked.

And Mom said, "Not quite. Over the bridge."

Which *is* far. It's ages. Because you have to go on the bus, or at least on a bike.

"Why has he gone?" Suzanne asked.

And Mom said, "I don't know."

I asked, "How long has he gone for?"

And Mom said, "I don't know."

And Suzanne said, "What about his rabbit?"

And Mom said, "For goodness' sake, girls, I don't *know!*"

And I told Mom she should have let me and Suzanne go with her to Joe's house, because she had hardly found out anything about Joe, or his rabbit. Because she hadn't asked the right questions. And she probably only asked Joe's Mom about work, and the weather, and washing, and things like that.

So I said, "Come on, Suzanne."

And Mom said, "Where are you going?"

And I said, "To see Joe-down-the-street's Mom to ask her when Joe will be coming back, and what is going to happen with his rabbit while he's gone, of course."

And Mom said, "No, Anna, you are not. Here, have an ice pop. Go out the back. And don't bother anyone, *especially* not Joe's Mom."

So me and Suzanne went outside with our ice pops. And we climbed up on the shed roof and ate them up there. And when they were finished, we lay flat on our backs to see how long we could stare at the sun. Graham Roberts says if you stare straight at the sun, you go blind. But me and Suzanne tried it one day, at exactly the same time, so

that if we did go blind, it would be together. And afterward we could still see fine. When we told Graham Roberts, he said we mustn't have stared for long enough.

Anyway, we didn't stare very long this time because there were too many clouds so it didn't count. So we sat up and dangled our legs over the edge of the shed instead. And we tried to think of things to do. Which was hard, because the rope swing was broken and we weren't allowed to do Spy Club or Mountain Rescue, or Dingo the Dog, or go on the Super-Speed-Bike-Machine. And we were sick of doing Worm Club and Bug Club and Shed Club and all that.

Suzanne said she wondered what Joe was doing now. And I said I wondered too. Because even though we hadn't done anything with Joe for ages I didn't really mind not doing things with Joe when I knew that he was down the road, guarding his rabbit. But now that I didn't know *what* Joe was doing, or when he was coming back, I couldn't stop wondering. Like when Mom gave my old teddy to Mrs. Constantine for the Sunday School Jumble Sale. Because before she gave it away, I forgot I even had it. But afterward I kept thinking about the teddy all the time, and how it was mine, and how it was meant to be in my toy box, and how I wanted it back.

Suzanne said we should never have told my Mom about Joe's Dad and his van and the boxes and all that. Because before we told her, we could have gone and asked Joe's Mom whatever questions we wanted. But now we couldn't because Mom had said we were banned.

We got down off the shed because it was starting to rain. And we went inside the shed, and sat on the boxes, and listened to the rain on the roof, and wondered about Joe, and what he was up to, and whether anything bad had happened to his rabbit since he had gone. And I said I thought it probably hadn't, because Joe only went about an hour ago, and Suzanne said I was probably right, but it would be nice to know for certain. Which was true. Then there was a knock on the shed door.

Suzanne looked through the spy hole (which is a knot in the wood that you can pop in and out).

"It's Tom," she said.

Tom put his eye to the spy hole and said, "Hello."

Suzanne said, "What's the password?"

"I don't know," said Tom. "What is it?"

And then me and Suzanne remembered
we had forgotten to make one up. Which we
never normally do because making up the
password is the first
rule of Shed Club.

So Suzanne told
Tom to guess.

And Tom guessed, "Open sesame."

Which is what he always says, and
Suzanne said, "Yes."

And Tom was very pleased, because
"Open sesame" had never been right
before.

We let Tom in, and we told him all about
Joe, and how he had got in the van with his
Dad, and the boxes, and how he got out
again. And how his Dad had driven away.
And how Joe chased his Dad down the road.
And how they drove away together. And
how he didn't take his rabbit with him. And

85

how Mom said Joe had gone to stay with his Dad, in an apartment, over the bridge. And how we didn't know why, or for how long, or what was going to happen to Joe's rabbit. And Suzanne said that she didn't think Joe wanted to go. And I said that he didn't want to leave his rabbit.

And Tom said, "Joe didn't want to go, and he didn't want to leave his rabbit, but he really, really, really didn't want to be left behind."

And Tom was probably right, because being left behind is one of Tom's worst things, so he knows all about it.

Because, when Tom was little, if Mom wanted to go somewhere without him, Dad had to take Tom out of the house first so that Tom was the one doing the leaving, not the one being left. Otherwise, if Tom was in the house and he found out that Mom had gone

somewhere and left him behind, he would stand at the door and look through the letter box and cry until she came home.

But the thing about taking Tom out, even just to the shops, is that you have to do a lot of other things on the way, like talking to Mr. Tucker, and walking on the wall, and wetting your wellies in the horse trough. So that's why, if Mom only wants to buy an onion or something, she tries to sneak out before Tom notices.

And then she runs down the road as fast as she can. Most of the time Mom doesn't get that far, though, because, like

she says, "Tom has got supersonic ears."
And he nearly always hears the
door handle turn, even from
upstairs.

And then he runs
down, quick, and puts
his wellies on, and says,
"Are you going out?"

And Mom says, "Oh,
for goodness' sake, Tom, I'm only going to
get an onion."

And Tom says, "I'll come."

And she has to take him with her. Because
if she doesn't, Tom gets what Nana used to
call "The Screaming Habdabs," where he
screams, and cries, and bangs his fists on
the door, and dribbles all over the doormat.

Anyway, me and Suzanne told Tom how
we wanted to know why Joe had gone to
his Dad's, and when he was coming back,

and what was going to happen to his rabbit while he was gone. And how we couldn't ask Joe's Mom about it because Mom had said we were banned.

And Tom said, "*I'm* not banned."

Which was true. So we decided that Tom should go instead. And Suzanne said we better make sure Tom knew exactly what to ask Joe's Mom first, before he went. And she wrote it all down on the notepad.

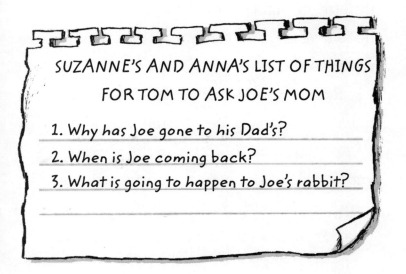

SUZANNE'S AND ANNA'S LIST OF THINGS
FOR TOM TO ASK JOE'S MOM

1. Why has Joe gone to his Dad's?
2. When is Joe coming back?
3. What is going to happen to Joe's rabbit?

Tom looked at the list for a while, and then he said, "What does it say?"

Because even though Tom goes to school, and he knows all his letters, he's only in kindergarten, and he doesn't really know what the letters say when you put them all together. So I said that Suzanne should just tell Tom what to say, and Tom would remember. And Tom said that was a good idea, because even though he isn't a very good *reader* yet, he is a *very* good rememberer. So that is what we did.

"Right," Suzanne said. "The shed is Joe's house, and Anna is Joe's Mom."

And Tom had to go out of the shed and knock on the door. And I answered it as Joe's Mom. And Suzanne told Tom exactly what he should say. And this is how it went:

Tom: "Hello."

Me being Joe's Mom: "Hello."

Tom: "How are you?"

Me being Joe's Mom: "Fine."

Tom: "Why has Joe gone to his Dad's?"

Me being Joe's Mom: "For a vacation."

Tom: "When will he be coming back?"

Me being Joe's Mom: "On Thursday."

Tom: "What about his rabbit?"

Me being Joe's Mom: "He will be back in a minute to take it with him."

Tom: "Thank you, Joe's Mom. Bye."

We practiced it again and again. And Suzanne told me to say different answers every time because she said, "Who knows what answers Joe's Mom might say."

Which was true. And she said it was best for Tom to get used to Joe's Mom saying all sorts of answers so he wouldn't get flustered and forget everything if she said something he didn't expect. We practiced it over and over again until Tom said all the questions exactly right, every time.

And, after about a million times, Suzanne said, "Tom is ready."

And Tom was pleased, because he said, "I'm a *very* good rememberer."

And we went off down the road.

Tom knocked on Joe's door. And me and Suzanne crouched behind the hedge.

And Joe's Mom answered the door and said, "Hello, Tom." Just like we thought.

And Tom said, "Hello, Joe's Mom. How are you?" Just like he was supposed to.

And Joe's Mom said, "Oh, I don't know, Tom, not very good."

And Tom said, "Oh."

And then he said, "Can I have a cookie?"

Which he was not supposed to say.

And Joe's Mom said, "Umm . . . Have you had your lunch?"

And Tom said, "No."

And Joe's Mom said, "You shouldn't really."

And Tom said, "Just a plain one."

And Joe's Mom said, "Okay."

And she went in the house and she brought the cookies out and she said, "Shall I have one with you?"

And Tom said, "Have you had your lunch?"

And Joe's Mom said, "No."

And Tom said, "Okay."

And they sat down on the doorstep. And they got a cookie each. And Tom had a bite of his cookie. And Joe's Mom had a bite of her cookie. And

Tom had a bite of his cookie. And Joe's Mom had a bite of her cookie. And they took turns having bites like that until their cookies were finished.

And then Tom said, "Shall we have a story?"

And Joe's Mom said, "Okay."

And she went and got some books, and Tom picked *Peter Rabbit* because, he said, "*Peter Rabbit* is one of my favorites."

And Joe's Mom said it was one of Joe's favorites too, when he was Tom's age. And they sat on the step. And Joe's Mom read *Peter Rabbit*. And when it was finished, they had another cookie, and they took it in turn to have bites.

And then Tom said, "Shall we have *Peter Rabbit* again?"

And Joe's Mom said, "All right."

And she read *Peter Rabbit* again. And she cuddled Tom in, and rubbed her cheek on his head. When the story was finished, Tom said, "That was nice."

And Joe's Mom said, "Yes."

And Tom said, "I'm going home now."

And Joe's Mom said, "Okay."

And she brushed the cookie crumbs off Tom, and off herself. And she smiled and said, "Don't tell about the cookies." And she put her finger over her mouth. And Tom put his finger over his mouth too. And he walked down the path, and back up the road.

And me and Suzanne followed, and I said, "Tom! You didn't ask why Joe has gone to his Dad's, and when he's coming back, and what's going to happen with his rabbit!"

And Tom said, "I forgot to remember. I had a story instead."

And I said, *"Tom!"*

And Tom said, "I didn't have cookies."

And then he said, "Joe's Mom cried on my head."

And she had as well, because Tom's hair was all wet.

Me and Suzanne went back to the shed and decided to wait until Monday at school,

when we could ask *Joe* why he had gone to his Dad's, and when he was coming back, and what was going to happen with his rabbit.

❝ CHAPTER 8 ❞
The Spare Seat

Most of the time I'm not very good at getting ready in the mornings. And that's why Mom always shouts things up the stairs like, "Anna, if you don't hurry up, I'm going to come up there and dress you myself."

But the Monday after Joe-down-the-street went away with his Dad in the van, I got ready really fast. And I packed my bag and got my uniform ready the night before. Because, like Suzanne said, "We have to get there early to talk to Joe before the bell rings."

I was eating my
breakfast when
the walkie-talkie
crackled, "Suzanne to
Anna. Suzanne to Anna. Are
you ready? Over."

"Anna to Suzanne. Anna
to Suzanne. Just finishing my
cornflakes. Over."

"Copy that," Suzanne said.
"Cornflakes. I'm putting my coat on. I'll
be out the back. Waiting on the wall. Over
and out."

And I ran and brushed my teeth, and got
my bag, and my coat, and Tom.

It's good talking on the walkie-talkies
in the mornings. Better than ringing on the
doorbell like most people have to. It would
be even better if we could take the walkie-
talkies to school, but Mom says she doesn't

think Mrs. Peters would like it, so we have to leave them at home.

When we got to the crossing, me and Suzanne and Tom were the first ones to arrive.

The Lollipop Lady said, "The early bird catches the worm, eh?" We call her that  because her sign looks like a lollipop.

Tom said, "I don't like worms."

"No?" said the Lollipop Lady.

"They wriggle my skin," Tom said.

"Fair enough," said the Lollipop Lady. "Some like carrots and others like cabbage."

"Come on," I said, "we've got to go."

And the Lollipop Lady said, "Time is money," and took us over the road.

Tom loves talking to the Lollipop Lady. Sometimes he talks to her for ages. But we didn't have time to talk to the Lollipop Lady for long that day, because we needed to get into the playground, to wait for Joe, to find out why he had gone to his Dad's and when he was coming home, and what was going to happen to his rabbit and all that.

Me and Suzanne and Tom were the first ones in the playground. After a while other people started coming in: the ones who walk, and the ones on bikes, and the ones from the bus, and Graham Roberts on his Grandad's tractor. Graham Roberts comes to school in all sorts of ways. On his brother's motorbike, and his cousin's combine harvester, and once with his Nan on her electric shopping scooter. But

Joe-down-the-street didn't arrive at all. And then the bell rang, and everyone went inside.

Mrs. Peters said, "Right, Class Five. Coats on pegs, bags down, bottoms on seats."

There was a space next to Emma Hendry, where Joe always sits.

When everyone was quiet, Mrs. Peters said that she had "an announcement to make," which means she had something to say. And she said that Joe wasn't coming to school this week, because he was going to go to another school, which was a very nice one, just like ours, in another village, on the other side of the bridge, and he was going to see if he liked it there. And if he *didn't* like it, he was going to come back to our school after Easter, and if he did like it, he was going to stay.

Emma Hendry put her hand up, and

Mrs. Peters said, "Yes, Emma?"

And Emma said, "Can I take the attendance sheet to the office when it's Joe's turn?"

And Mrs. Peters said, "No, because if he's not here, Joe won't have a turn, will he?"

And Suzanne said, "Won't you say Joe's name?"

And Mrs. Peters said, "No."

And I said, "What about when Joe comes back?"

And Mrs. Peters said, "If Joe comes back, I will say his name again."

And then she said, "Hands up who knows whose will be the last name on the attendance sheet now."

And Emma Hendry put her hand up.

"Jake Upton?"

And Jake Upton said, "Shelly Wainwright is after me."

And Mrs. Peters said, "That's right. Shelly Wainwright, you will be last on the attendance sheet."

And Shelly Wainwright said, "I don't want to be last. I like being second to last."

And Mrs. Peters said, "Well, that's the way the alphabet works."

Emma Hendry asked, "Who is going to sit in Joe's seat next to me if he's not coming back?"

And Suzanne said, "He probably is coming back, because he's left the New Rabbit behind."

And I said, "Yes, because Joe lives down the same road as me and Suzanne."

Graham Roberts said, "That's probably why he went away."

And I said, "No, it isn't."

And Graham Roberts said, "Yes, it is."

And I said, "No, it isn't."

And Graham Roberts said, "Yes, it is."

And I said, **"NO, IT ISN'T!"** And I kicked Graham Roberts under the table. And Graham Roberts kicked me back.

And Mrs. Peters said, "Excuse me! Anna Morris! I am not impressed! Graham Roberts, come and sit next to Emma Hendry, please."

Emma Hendry did not look very happy that Graham Roberts was going to sit next to her, because Graham Roberts swings on his chair, and copies other people's work, and puts their pencils up his nose. And Emma Hendry doesn't like those kinds of things. And also, Graham Roberts always tries to touch Emma Hendry's hair. And then Emma puts her hand up and

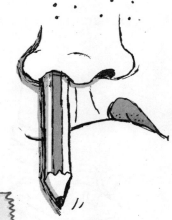

says, "Mrs. Peters, Graham Roberts is touching my hair again."

I wouldn't tell Mrs. Peters if Graham Roberts touched my hair.

Graham Roberts picked up his things and went to sit with Emma Hendry. And I wished I hadn't kicked him.

"Who's going to sit next to me?" I said.

"For the time being, Anna, you can sit by yourself. If you're good this week, I will have another think."

I undid my laces, and then I did them back up again. And I didn't say anything. Because everyone was looking. And because I didn't want to sit on my own. And

because no one can be good for a *week*. And because Joe-down-the-street was moving *schools* as *well* as houses, and no one had told us *that*. And if he still lived at his Mom's house, instead of ages away with his Dad, I wouldn't have to sit on my own, because there wouldn't be a spare seat next to Emma Hendry for Graham Roberts to go and sit in in the first place.

I wrote a note to Suzanne: **"What are we going to do about Joe-down-the-street?"**

Mrs. Peters said, "Anna, writing notes is *not* being good."

And she took the note from me. And she put it in the trash. And then she took roll. And she stopped at Shelly Wainwright.

After school Mrs. Peters said she had some pictures and work and things that she wanted me and Suzanne to take home to give to Joe next time he came to his Mom's.

Me and Suzanne put all Joe's work up on the walls in the shed. There were paintings and drawings and poems and stories and collages and cutouts and math problems and everything. And they were *all* about his rabbit.

I said, "How are we going to get Joe-down-the-street back?"

And Suzanne looked at all Joe's work on the walls. "I don't know," she said, "but it's got to be something to do with the New Rabbit."

🐾 CHAPTER 9 🐾
Keeping the Rabbit Alive

We didn't know how yet, but me and Suzanne were sure that the New Rabbit was the thing that could make Joe come back and live down the road. And that's why, even though Mom said we had to stay out of it, and stop sticking our noses in, me and Suzanne decided that we'd better start looking after the New Rabbit ourselves. Because if anything bad happened to the New Rabbit, like it died, then Joe would never come back. But while the New Rabbit

was here, there was a chance that he might.

Because me and Suzanne heard Joe's Mom talking to my Mom on the phone when we listened in upstairs. And Joe's Mom said Joe didn't really know *where* he wanted to live, or *what* he wanted to do. And the only reason he hadn't taken the New Rabbit with him to his Dad's was because the landlord at Joe's Dad's apartment had said, "No Pets Allowed."

Suzanne said she bet Joe was worrying about the New Rabbit all the time, now that no one was guarding it. Because even though Joe's Mom said Joe would be coming back for Easter, and weekends, and that sort of thing, it still meant the rabbit

was hardly ever getting guarded. And, like Joe always said, and like it shows on his pie chart, which we hung up in the shed, "The more time the rabbit gets guarded, the less chance there is of the rabbit getting got."

Joe's Mom told my Mom that she was going to look after the rabbit herself.

When Mom got off the phone, me and Suzanne put the other phone down and went downstairs.

"Who was on the phone?" I asked.

"Joe's Mom."

"Oh."

I said, "Why are no pets allowed at Joe's Dad's apartment?"

And Mom said, "Were you listening in again, Anna?"

I said, "No."

And Mom said, "Mmm."

I said, "I don't think Joe's Mom will be very good at looking after Joe's rabbit on her own."

"I'm sure Pam is quite capable of looking after a rabbit, Anna."

But me and Suzanne didn't think she was.

Because we had got the binoculars and the notepad out again and done some more spying. And for one thing, Joe's Mom was at work most of the time. And for another thing, she never went in the garden and marched up and down with the Super Soaker. And for an even other thing, she didn't give the rabbit anything to eat. Except millions of dry brown pellets. And you can't just eat those on their own.

Because, like Suzanne said, "Remember what happened when you tried to eat that whole pack of crackers?"

Which I had bet Suzanne I could. But in the end I could only eat two because I couldn't even swallow them down. And then a bit went down the wrong way, and I nearly choked to death. And Suzanne had to hit me on the head and throw cold water in my face. And the brown pellets that Joe's Mom gave the New Rabbit were even drier than crackers. Because I tried one.

I said I thought Suzanne was right, and anyway, even if it didn't choke to death, the New Rabbit shouldn't just eat pellets every day because, like Mom says, "You have to eat fruit and vegetables, Anna, or you will get scurvy and die, like a seventeenth-century sailor."

This is what it says in my dictionary about what scurvy is:

scurvy [skur-vee] ✦ *noun*
a disease marked by swollen and bleeding gums, livid spots on the skin, and suppurating wounds, due to a diet lacking in vitamin C

And this is what it says in Suzanne's dictionary:

scurvy [skur-vee] ✦ *noun*
a disease caused by a deficiency of ascorbic acid characterized by spongy gums, the opening of previously healed wounds, and bleeding from the mucous membranes

And we definitely didn't want Joe's rabbit to get that.

Me and Suzanne decided that as well as making sure it didn't choke to death, or die of scurvy, we'd better start guarding the New Rabbit, in case something else killed it, like the New Cat.

"It isn't just the New Cat that could get the New Rabbit either," I said, "because I looked on the computer, and *everything* wants to get rabbits, especially at night.

Dogs, and cats, and hawks, and owls, and weasels, and foxes, and farmers, and old ladies who want rabbits' fur for hats."

And Suzanne said, "I already knew that."

And then she said we should make a list of all the things we had to do to make sure the New Rabbit didn't die.

ANNA'S AND SUZANNE'S LIST OF THINGS TO DO TO MAKE SURE THE NEW RABBIT DOESN'T DIE

1. Put a bell on the New Cat's collar so it can't sneak up and scare the New Rabbit to death like it did with the Old Rabbit
2. Put Suzanne's little brother Carl's old baby monitor under the New Rabbit's hutch so we can hear if anything is happening
3. Guard the New Rabbit with Super Soakers
4. Feed the New Rabbit fruit and vegetables so it doesn't get scurvy and die
5. Throw the rabbit's pellets away so it doesn't choke to death

It took quite a long time trying to put a bell on the New Cat's collar. First of all we had to find one. So we went to see Mrs. Rotherham, and we told her all about how we needed to put a bell on the New Cat's collar to stop it from sneaking up on the New Rabbit and scaring it to death.

Mrs. Rotherham said, "I see. A Cat Attack Alarm . . . I wonder if I can lay my hands on a bell." And she went in her cupboard for ages until she did. And then we all had a bowl of ice cream.

And then we had to find the New Cat, and catch it, and then the New Cat attacked us, and then we had to find Tom, to ask him to put the Cat Attack Alarm on the New Cat for us, because he is friends with the New Cat, so it might not mind so much.

And at first Tom said, "No."

Because, he said, "I don't think the

New Cat would like to have a Cat Attack Alarm on."

And Suzanne said, "We'll give you some cookies."

So Tom said, "Okay."

And Suzanne pinched some cookies from her house, and I pinched some from ours, and we gave them to Tom. And Tom put the Cat Attack Alarm on the New Cat's collar. And the New Cat *didn't* want the Cat Attack Alarm on at all. She had a fight with it. But she didn't win, because the Cat Attack Alarm stayed on. Tom said he felt sorry for the New Cat. And he sat down and stroked the New Cat on the head so its ears went flat. And Tom ate all his cookies.

CHAPTER 10
The Tale of
the Fierce Bad Rabbit

The next day after school, while Joe-down-
the-street's Mom was still at work, me and
Suzanne went to see if Mrs. Rotherham

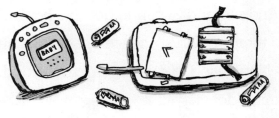

had any batteries to put in Carl's old baby
monitor. And we told her all about how we
needed it to listen out for Joe's New Rabbit

now that Joe wasn't down the road anymore.

Mrs. Rotherham said, "Of course. A Rabbit Monitor. No rabbit should be without one."

And she checked inside it and said, "Mmm . . . Four double A batteries. . . . I'll see if I can lay my hands on some."

And after ages in her cupboard, she did. And she put the batteries in the monitor, and she checked that it worked by leaving one end of the monitor with us and taking the other end upstairs and saying, "Help! Help! It's me, Mrs. Rotherham. I'm trapped in the baby monitor. Can anybody hear me?"

And me and Suzanne got The Hysterics. And then we had some ice cream. Because, like Nana used to say, ice cream is good for calming down.

And then we went down the road and put the listening part of the Rabbit Monitor on the shelf in the shed. And we put the

hearing part under the New Rabbit's hutch. And we peered in to have a look at the New Rabbit. There was a lot of hay in the way, all piled up against the wire mesh at the front. Suzanne reached her hand in through the hay and felt around.

"Oh," she said, "I can feel it. It's all soft, and fluffy, and warm."

And then she screamed, *"AGH!"* and she pulled her hand back. Her finger was bleeding. She put it in her mouth.

"It bit me!" she said.

I said, "Maybe it was asleep, and it got frightened when you put your hand in." Because when me and Tom had hamsters, our Hamster Manual said that hamsters only bite when they are frightened. And it's probably the same with rabbits.

So I said, "Things only bite when they're frightened."

121

And Suzanne said, "No, they don't. Some things bite because they like to."

And I said, "Like what?"

And Suzanne said, "Like the New Cat!"

"The New Cat is different," I said. "You don't get rabbits like that. Rabbits just hop around, and eat lettuce, and wear yellow ribbons on Easter cards and things."

Suzanne took her finger out of her mouth. It was still bleeding.

"You put *your* hand in its hutch, then."

"I will," I said.

I undid the latch, and opened the door a crack, and slowly put my hand in the hutch, lying it flat on the bottom, like the Hamster Manual said you should.

I heard something rustle, and then I felt the rabbit's fur

against my hand, and its whiskers, and its wet nose.

I kept very still.

"It's sniffing me," I said. "It tickles."

And then I said, "*Nice* New Rabbit."

And then I said, **"AGH!"**

And pulled my hand away. And put my finger in my mouth. **"It bit me!"**

"*See,*" Suzanne said.

And she put the latch back on.

The New Rabbit rustled in the hay. It pushed its way through to the front of the hutch. It was white. And it had pink eyes. And it was Absolutely Enormous. The New Rabbit stared out at us through the wire mesh.

Suzanne said, "Look at its eyes!"

And I said, "Look at its ears!"

And Suzanne said, "Look at its teeth!"

123

And I said, "Look at its claws!"

And Suzanne said, "When did it get so *big*?"

Because the last time me and Suzanne had seen the New Rabbit, it was tiny. And its eyes were closed. And it fitted inside Joe's hand.

The New Rabbit gnawed on the wire on the front of the hutch. It had long yellow teeth.

Suzanne said, "It's not like Joe's *Old* Rabbit, is it?"

And it wasn't, because if you put your hand in the Old Rabbit's hutch, the Old Rabbit would rub its head against you, and hop onto your hand to be taken out. And then, if you let it, it would go up your sweater and nuzzle your neck.

You couldn't fit the New Rabbit up your sweater. Not even if you wanted to. And you wouldn't want to anyway.

We stared at the New Rabbit. And the New Rabbit stared back at us.

Suzanne said, "It's too big for the hutch."

Which was true. It was almost as big as the hutch itself.

"Maybe that's why it looks angry," I said.

Because the Old Rabbit had lots of room to hop around. But if the New Rabbit stretched out, its feet would touch both ends of the hutch.

I said, "We could let it out for a bit."

And Suzanne said, "How will we get it back in?"

"We won't let it *out* out," I said. "We'll just let it out in the run. For a few minutes. And then we'll shoo it back in."

And Suzanne said, "Good idea."

Which Suzanne hardly ever says, so that meant it was.

We picked up the run from the corner of the garden and put it on the front of the hutch. And it fitted just right. Because that's how Joe's Dad had made it, ages ago, for the Old Rabbit, when he still lived with Joe and Joe's Mom.

There was a small hole in the wire mesh, in one corner of the run. We looked at the hole, and we looked at the rabbit. The hole was about the size of a jam jar. And the rabbit was about the size of a dog. In fact, it was bigger than a dog. It was bigger than

Miss Matheson's dog, anyway, because that's only the same size as a guinea pig.

"The rabbit can't fit through the hole," I said.

← Rabbit

←Hole

"No, definitely not," said Suzanne.

So we opened the door of the hutch. And the rabbit hopped out into the run. And it stood very still in the middle of the run, and it sniffed the air, and it put its ears right up. And then it hopped over to the corner with the hole. And it looked at the hole. And then, in a second, it squeezed through it.

Suzanne said, **"It's out!"**

And I said, "The gate!"

I ran to the gate and slammed it shut. The

rabbit looked angrier than ever. It thumped its back leg on the ground. I tried to grab the rabbit. And Suzanne tried to grab the rabbit. But whenever we got near it, the New Rabbit ran at us and scrabbled and scratched and tried to bite.

I said, "We need gardening gloves." Like Mom uses to put the New Cat in its carrying case to take it to the vet.

And I ran up the road to the shed to get them.

When I got back, Suzanne was running round Joe's garden in circles, and the New Rabbit was running after her.

"Suzanne," I said. "Turn around and run at the rabbit, to shoo it toward me. I'll get it with the gardening gloves."

And she did.

I grabbed hold of the rabbit. It scrabbled

and scratched and clawed and kicked. But I held on to it, tight.

And then I felt it bite. My blood came right through the gardening gloves. I dropped the rabbit. And ran up the road with my finger in my mouth.

I got a Band-Aid from the house for my hand. And I went into the shed and got my big brother Andy's football pads and his bike helmet. I put them on. And I put his mouth guard in my mouth. I took his shin guards, some old oven mitts, and a balaclava for Suzanne. And I got two fishing nets.

When I got back, Suzanne was in the corner of Joe's garden, pressed against the fence, and the New Rabbit was in front of her, and it was making a growling sound. There were scratches all over Suzanne's legs.

I said, "I didn't know rabbits growled."

And Suzanne said, **"HELP!"**

"You need to get to the gate!"

"I can't! I'm stuck."

"Jump!" I said.

Suzanne jumped right over the rabbit and ran for the gate. And when she got through it, she slammed it shut. I gave Suzanne the shin guards, and the oven mitts, and the mouth guard and the balaclava.

And she put them on.

Then we got The Hysterics because we looked quite funny, and we had to lie down on the pavement for a bit.

And then we stopped having The Hysterics, because it wasn't funny really, because, like Suzanne said, "This is *serious*."

So we went back in.

The rabbit stood still in the middle of the grass, sniffing the air, with its enormous ears up. We took a step toward it, and it thumped its back leg on the ground, and growled again.

"Ready?" I said.

And Suzanne said, "Yes."

We ran at the New Rabbit, and we tried to catch it under the fishing nets, but the New Rabbit was too quick. And the fishing nets were too small. And it hopped and jumped and ran all around the garden, and the more we chased it, the farther away it got.

And then, suddenly, the New Rabbit stopped, and it got up on its hind legs, and it put its ears right up, and it sniffed the air.

And it stared at the gate. And it froze.

The gate started to open. And I thought me and Suzanne were in Big Trouble then, because it was probably Joe's Mom.

But it wasn't. It was Tom. And he wasn't on his own. He was with the New Cat.

When it saw the New Rabbit, the New Cat's eyes went very wide, and it got down very low. And it stared at the New Rabbit. And the New Rabbit got down low too and stared back at the New Cat. And they stayed very still.

And the rabbit went, **"Ggrrrrrrrr."**
And the cat went, *"Ttsssss"*

And then the New Rabbit turned and shot back through the hole in the run and up into its hutch. And Suzanne closed the door, and I fastened the latch.

When I got home, Mom said, "Anna, where did you get all those scratches?"

And I said, "From Suzanne."

CHAPTER 11
Rabbit Food

After that, even though me and Suzanne decided we didn't really like the New Rabbit, we started looking after it all the time. We sat on the pavement outside Joe's house with Super Soakers, and we took turns to take the Rabbit Monitor to bed at night. We fed the New Rabbit every morning on the way to school, and every

afternoon on the way back. And
at first we put in things we found
at home, but then Mom said, "I could
have sworn I had some spinach."

And, "Has anyone seen the
celery?"

And, "How can you *lose* a *leek*?"

And when Suzanne's Dad said,

**"WHAT ON EARTH HAS HAPPENED TO ALL
MY HERBS?"** we started getting things
from other places instead.

We got apples from Mr. Tucker's
tree, and cress from the window
ledge in the classroom at school,
and privet leaves from Miss
Matheson's hedge.

And we wanted to get the

parsley from Miss Matheson's back garden too. But Miss Matheson kept spotting us and tapping on her window, saying, **"Private property! Private property! I won't have my plants purloined!"**

And then she phoned Mom to complain.

This is what it says in my dictionary about purloining . . .

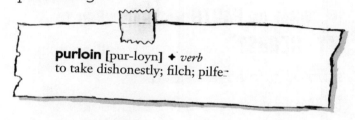

purloin [pur-loyn] ✦ *verb*
to take dishonestly; filch; pilfer

This is what it said in Suzanne's dictionary . . .

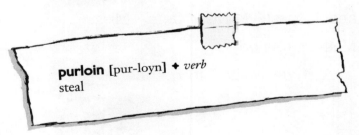

purloin [pur-loyn] ✦ *verb*
steal

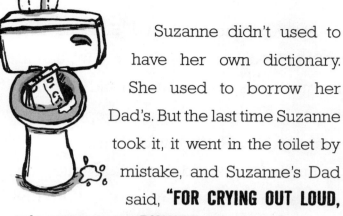

Suzanne didn't used to have her own dictionary. She used to borrow her Dad's. But the last time Suzanne took it, it went in the toilet by mistake, and Suzanne's Dad said, **"FOR CRYING OUT LOUD, IT'S COMPLETELY RUINED, SUZANNE!"** And he threw it in the trash.

He bought a new dictionary, and he said, **"IF YOU GO ANYWHERE NEAR IT, SUZANNE, YOUR LIFE WILL NOT BE WORTH LIVING!"**

But Suzanne didn't need to go anywhere near it anyway, because we got the old dictionary out of the bin and dried it out in our airing cupboard, and stuck the pages that had torn back together, and now it's as good as before, except the pages are a bit wobbly and it smells a bit strange.

Anyway, when me and Suzanne first started feeding the New Rabbit, we had to be quick getting our hands in and out of the hutch, because as soon as we opened the latch, the New Rabbit attacked us.

But on the second day it didn't bite, and on the third day it let us stroke it. And at first we thought it was because the New Rabbit was starting to like us. But on the fourth day, when the New Rabbit didn't even get up, and hardly opened its eyes, Suzanne said, "I don't think the New Rabbit is very well."

And I said that I didn't think it was either. Because its fur looked funny, and it had red patches all over its chest.

When we told Tom all about how the New Rabbit was sick, Tom said, "When Peter Rabbit is poorly, Mrs. Rabbit gives him chamomile tea."

Me and Suzanne looked in the cupboards in Suzanne's kitchen, and then we looked in the cupboards in my kitchen, but we couldn't find any chamomile tea. We did find some other tea, though, which it said on the box was "made only with the finest tips." Which we thought would be just as good.

I'm not supposed to make hot drinks because, once, I tried to make coffee, and I forgot to put water in the kettle, and I put half a jar of coffee granules in instead, and when I turned it on, the kettle made a fizzing noise and went **BANG!** And that's why there's a big black patch on the kitchen counter.

So we made the tea very quickly, and went outside and waited for it to cool, and then we took it down the road and we tipped the New Rabbit's water out of its bowl and we poured the tea in instead. Then we went back to the shed.

And after a while Mom came and she knocked on the door and she said, "Have you been using the kettle again and trying to make tea in the kitchen?"

And I said, "No."

And Mom said, "Mmm."

And then she said, "What are you two *up* to?"

And Suzanne said, "Nothing."

And Mom said, "Mmm."

And then she said that Joe-down-the-street was coming home tomorrow for Easter, and that me and Suzanne should call on him and try to be kind, and that we should do the things Joe wanted, even if it was boring, like guarding his rabbit.

‌CHAPTER 12 ‌
Joe's Down the Street Again

In the morning, when Joe's Dad's van pulled into the road, me and Suzanne were standing at Joe's gate with our Super Soakers.

Joe and his Dad got out. Joe's Dad said, "Armed guard, eh, girls?"

And we said, "Yes."

"Can't be too careful," he said, and he held up his hands, and we let him pass, and he went inside. And me and Suzanne told Joe all about how we had been guarding the New Rabbit, in secret, and how we had put the Cat Attack Alarm on the New Cat's collar so it couldn't sneak up and scare the New Rabbit to death, and we showed him the Rabbit Monitor, under the hutch, and told him how the other end was in the shed, and how at night we took turns  taking it to bed so we would hear if anything happened.

But we didn't tell him about how we had let the New Rabbit out by mistake, or how the New Cat had seen it, or how Joe's Mom was only giving it bowls of brown pellets, and how we had to feed it ourselves, because like Mom said to us before we left the house, "Don't go worrying Joe about his rabbit."

Joe looked in at the New Rabbit, and he

opened the hutch, and he put his hand in and pushed back some of the straw.

"I don't think the New Rabbit is very well," he said. "Normally, the New Rabbit bites."

"Oh," I said.

"Does it?" said Suzanne.

And we pulled our sleeves over our hands to cover our scratches and Band-Aids.

Joe looked in the hutch again. He said that the New Rabbit's poos were all wrong, because they're supposed to be small and hard, not wet and stuck to its bum. Then he looked at the New Rabbit's chest. And he said its fur had gone strange, and it didn't normally have red patches like that.

And then Joe's Dad came out of the

house. And he mended the hole in the wire in the rabbit run. And he went to the van, and he got a paper bag out, and he gave it to Joe.

And he said, "I've told your Mom about the medicine. Don't forget to take it, champ."

And Joe said, "No."

Joe's Dad gave him a cuddle. And he scrubbed him on the head. And he got in the van and drove away.

Joe watched the van go.

"What medicine?" said Suzanne.

Joe showed her. There was a tube of cream, and a bottle of liquid. The tube

said FLORASONE and the bottle said IMODIUM.

Suzanne looked at the bottle, and at the tube. And then she looked at the rabbit. And then she looked at Joe.

And then she said, "You and the rabbit are *both* poorly."

And Joe said, "Yes."

And then Joe's Mom came out. And she kissed Joe all over his face until Joe went red. And then she said, "Sorry, Joe." And then she kissed him again.

Joe told his Mom that he thought the New Rabbit was poorly.

And Joe's Mom said that she knew, and that she was keeping a close eye on the rabbit, and she checked the New Rabbit's chest, and she looked in its mouth and she said, "He hasn't been himself. I've spoken to the vet, and if he's not any better tomorrow, we'll take him to see her."

And then she lifted up Joe's T-shirt, and she looked at *his* chest too, and it had a red rash all over it, and she looked in his mouth. And she said, "And if *you* aren't any better tomorrow, we'll take you to the vet as well."

And she kissed Joe again. And then she said that her and Joe were going to have some lunch.

And me and Suzanne said that if Joe wanted, he could come up to the shed after, and we would let him be in our clubs.

On the way up the road, Suzanne said, "Let's go on the computer and look something up." Which Suzanne never normally wants to do.

We sat down at the screen, and Suzanne put in "Florasone," and it said, "**Florasone: a cream for eczema.**"

And then she put in
"Imodium," and it said,
**"Imodium: for upset
stomachs and diarrhea."**

And then she put in "diarrhea and
eczema" and she said, "Let's print these
pages off."

I went and asked Mom. I'm not allowed
to print things without asking anymore,
after I printed off two hundred and forty-
three pages for Tom about Batman and
Bob the Builder.

Mom came with the printer cable,
and she looked at the screen and she
said, "Why do you want to
print off descriptions of
eczema and diarrhea?"

"It's for Suzanne," I
said.

Suzanne scratched her chest and rubbed her stomach. "I'm not well," she said.

Mom said, "Mmm," and pressed print.

Suzanne put the pages in her pocket.

And Mom made us some cheese sand-wiches and some squash, and we took them out to the shed, and we ate our sandwiches and read what it said about eczema and diarrhea.

Suzanne said, "Joe and the New Rabbit have got exactly the same things wrong with them."

"Have they?"

"Yes. At exactly the same time."

"Oh."

"Both of them were fine before Joe went away."

"So?" I said.

And Suzanne said, *"So . . . "*

I asked Suzanne if she wanted the rest of her sandwich.

And Suzanne said, "No."

So I had it instead. And I said, "It's probably a coincidence."

"It *could* be a coincidence," Suzanne said. "But it could be *connected*."

"Why?"

"Because," Suzanne said, "Joe and the New Rabbit were both fine. And then Joe and the New Rabbit got separated. And that's when Joe and the New Rabbit got poorly. So now that Joe and the New Rabbit are back together again, what's going to happen?"

"I don't know," I said. Because I hate riddles and things like that because I never know the answer.

"They might both get better again. And if they do, it can't just be a coincidence, can it? It has to be connected."

149

And I said, "I don't know." Because I didn't.

This is what it says a "coincidence" is in my dictionary:

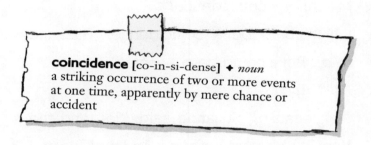

coincidence [co-in-si-dense] ✦ *noun*
a striking occurrence of two or more events at one time, apparently by mere chance or accident

This it what it says "connected" is in my dictionary:

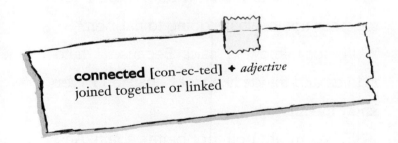

connected [con-ec-ted] ✦ *adjective*
joined together or linked

I didn't know if Joe and the New Rabbit being poorly with the same thing at the same time was a coincidence, or if it was connected, but I was glad we didn't have to look after the New Rabbit for two weeks while Joe was back down the road for Easter.

Because it's quite hard work, looking after a rabbit. Especially when you aren't supposed to be looking after it, and you have to do it in secret, and hide behind the hedge to guard it, and steal all its food for it, and listen to it on the Rabbit Monitor in bed every other night.

Now that Joe was back to look after his rabbit himself, me and Suzanne could do all the other things that we used to do before we had to look after the New Rabbit all the time.

So I said, "Let's do something."

And Suzanne said, "What?"

"I don't know."

We sat on the roof and tried to think.

And Suzanne said she wondered what Joe was doing now. And whether he had finished his lunch.

And I said so did I.

And Suzanne said she wondered if Joe would come up to the shed.

And I said that he probably wouldn't, because he would probably just go back to guarding his rabbit all the time.

And then we saw Joe coming up the back lane.

And we got down from the roof, and we told Joe the password, and we let him in the shed, and we showed him how we had put all his work up on the walls, and how we had the Rabbit Monitor on the shelf to listen out for the New Rabbit. And Joe looked pretty pleased.

"Shall we play Dingo the Dog?" I said.

At first Joe didn't want to, but Suzanne gave him the Rabbit Monitor to put in his pocket so he could hear if anything happened. And then he said, "Okay."

And Suzanne went and got Barney's old collar and leash, and we went out the back and played Dingo the Dog.

And afterward we went to Joe's house, and we played Mountain Rescue. And Joe's Mom got us fish and chips. And she said me and Suzanne could stay the night, if we liked. And we did.

So we went home to

get our pajamas and toothbrushes and all that.

And Suzanne told Joe about how it isn't as good in Mrs. Peters's class without him. And how Shelly Wainwright is last on the attendance sheet, and how she doesn't like being last because she liked being second to last, like she was when Joe was there.

And I told Joe about how Mrs. Peters made Graham Roberts move and sit in Joe's seat, and how I had to sit on my own, and I didn't like it. And I said that it was probably much better at Joe's new school.

But Joe said it wasn't, because he liked Mrs. Peters because she didn't mind him not putting his hand up, and doing all his work about rabbits and everything, but his new teacher did mind. And everyone called him Joseph instead of Joe.

And Suzanne said, "Mrs. Peters said you could come back to our school after Easter if you didn't like it at your new one."

And Joe said, "I can't, because after Mom shouted at me about always guarding the New Rabbit, I shouted back and said, **"I WANT TO LIVE WITH DAD!"** And Mom said that I could if I really wanted to. And I said I did. And I phoned Dad and he said that he would come and get me in the morning. And when the morning came, I didn't want to go, but I had to then because that's what I'd said. And I didn't want Dad to think I didn't want to live with him." Which is like when I went to live with Mrs. Rotherham. When I didn't really want to. Before Tom came to rescue me.

And then Joe showed us a list that he had done, and it said:

GOOD THINGS ABOUT LIVING
WITH MY DAD:

I see my Dad every day

BAD THINGS ABOUT LIVING WITH MY DAD:

The New Rabbit isn't there

The food

My bed

There's no one to play with

Dad's New Girlfriend

I don't like the school

Mom isn't there

And then Joe drew us a picture of his Dad's apartment, and where his bedroom is at the back, and how you get there.

You go down our road and past the horse trough, and the shops, and the Bottom Bus Stop, and over the bridge and round the roundabout, and down the track, and through the old tunnel, and through the gate, and across the field, and then you're there.

And Joe said that maybe me and Suzanne could come and see him soon, after school.

And Suzanne said that we probably couldn't, because it was way past the Bottom Bus Stop and everything, which is Out-of-Bounds.

And Joe said, "You could come on the Super-Speed-Bike-Machine, and bring me back on the stunt pegs."

And I said how we weren't allowed to get the Super-Speed-Bike-Machine out anymore after we went into the road and Tom hit his head and had to have six sticky stitches.

And Joe said, "Oh."

And then he wrote, "Map to Joe's Dad's apartment" on the top of the paper. And he said we could have it anyway, just in case.

And I said we would pin it on the wall in the shed. And we would go when we were old enough.

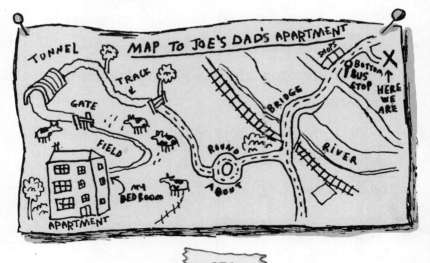

And Joe said I should put the list of things he didn't like about living with his Dad in the shed as well, because he didn't want his Dad to see it.

So I folded the list and the map up, and I put them in my bag.

And then Suzanne started making funny noises and opening and closing her mouth. And snoring. And I held her nose, and me and Joe got The Hysterics.

And Suzanne woke up and said it wasn't funny, actually, because she couldn't help it and she might have to have her adenoids out.

This is what it says about adenoids in my dictionary:

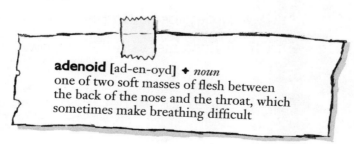

adenoid [ad-en-oyd] ✦ *noun*
one of two soft masses of flesh between the back of the nose and the throat, which sometimes make breathing difficult

In the morning me and Suzanne and Joe-down-the-street played Mountain Rescue again, and Dingo the Dog, and Tom played too. And we sat on the shed roof and did other things, like seeing how long we could stare at the sun before we went blind, and how long we could hold our breath before we died, and talking about the Super-Speed-Bike-Machine.

And after that, as soon as he had finished his breakfast and looked after his rabbit, Joe came up the road to meet me and Suzanne every day.

And every day Suzanne said, "How's the New Rabbit?"

And every day Joe said, "Better."

And then Suzanne said, "And how are *you*?"

And Joe looked at her a bit funny,

because it's not like Suzanne is always asking people how they are or anything.

And he said, "I'm better too."

And Suzanne kept looking at Joe's chest and asking him about his poo. And looking in on the New Rabbit and checking its poos and its chest too. And when Joe wasn't looking, she wrote it all down in the Spy Club notebook: 10:00 a.m., Tuesday. Joe much better. Rabbit much better too.

And she said to me, "Joe and the rabbit are getting better every day."

And I said, "So?"

And Suzanne said, "They were both fine, and then when Joe went away, they both got poorly. And now that Joe is back, they are both fine again."

And then she said, "It *can't* just be a coincidence."

‏CHAPTER 13 ‏

Purloining Miss Matheson's Parsley

The day Joe gave us the Rabbit Monitor back and left to go to his Dad's, me and Suzanne promised him we would keep looking after the New Rabbit.

So that afternoon we collected privet leaves and daffodils. And then we got the binoculars and the Spy Club notebook out of the shed and we started to spy on Miss Matheson because

even though we were banned, we had to get some of her parsley for the New Rabbit in case it got poorly again, because, like Tom said, "Before the chamomile tea, Peter Rabbit eats some parsley to make him feel better."

We looked over Miss Matheson's fence with the binoculars.

And Suzanne wrote down in the note-book:

2:45 p.m.–Miss Matheson digging her parsley up
3:15 p.m.–Miss Matheson putting parsley on her compost heap
3:30 p.m.–Miss Matheson going into her house

We sneaked in over the gate, and we ran to the compost heap and took as much of the parsley as we could carry, and we put it in the shed. The parsley that grows in Miss Matheson's garden is just like normal parsley, except much taller, and fatter, and it smells strange. And then we shut the shed, and locked the padlock, and we went down the road with the privet leaves and the daffodils and a little piece of parsley.

The New Rabbit was back to how it used to be, before Joe left, and it tried to bite us when we put our hands in.

We sat and watched it eat the privet and the daffodils. And we gave it the little bit of parsley, just to make sure.

And I said, "Maybe the New Rabbit is going to be fine."

And Suzanne said, "Maybe."

❦ CHAPTER 14 ❦
Till Death Do Us Part

In the morning it was the first day back at school, and me and Suzanne and Tom looked in on the New Rabbit on the way, and gave it some more of the parsley to eat, but the rabbit didn't try to bite. It was just lying still again.

Suzanne said, "The rabbit was fine, and then Joe went away and the rabbit was poorly. And then Joe came back, and the rabbit got better. And now Joe has gone away again and the rabbit is poorly again. It *can't* be a coincidence."

And I said, "It *has* to be connected."

We must have fed the rabbit for too long because Suzanne looked at her watch and jumped up and said, "It's five to nine!"

I haven't got a watch because I lost mine, and anyway, like Suzanne says, even when I did have one, it didn't help because I'm not very good at telling the time.

We closed the hutch and fastened the latch and ran as fast as we could, and at first we thought the Lollipop Lady had gone home because she wasn't standing at the crossing. But when we got closer, we saw she was sitting on the bench, under the chestnut tree, reading a paper.

The Lollipop Lady stood up, and a gust of wind whipped her newspaper out of her hands, and the pages went everywhere and

she ran around trying to grab them.

"Well, if it's not one thing, it's another," she said.

And me and Suzanne and Tom ran around as well, picking up the pages, and we gave them all back, except I saw Suzanne take one page and fold it up and put it in her pocket.

And Suzanne said, "We're late."

And the Lollipop Lady said, "Shake a leg, then."

And she took us over the road.

And we shouted, **"THANKS"** and went over the wall and into the playground.

And the Lollipop Lady shouted after us, "BETTER LATE THAN NEVER. BLAME IT ON THE RAIN!" even though it wasn't raining.

Tom ran to his classroom, and me and Suzanne ran to ours.

And Miss Peters looked at the clock and said, "What time do you call this?"

And I didn't know what time to call it because I can only do the o'clocks and the half pasts, and it wasn't one of those.

And Suzanne said she called it, "Quarter past nine."

And then she said, "The Lollipop Lady's newspaper blew away, and we had to help her catch it."

And Mrs. Peters said, "Mmm."

And then she said, "Sit down."

168

At recess, me and Suzanne went up into the top corner of the field, and Suzanne showed me the piece of newspaper that she had folded up and put in her pocket. It said:

WOMAN'S SHED NEARLY BURNS DOWN.

"Not that bit," said Suzanne. "Look!" And she pointed to the part underneath. It said:

CAN'T LIVE APART

Local couple Sidney and Edith Armstrong both died last week within hours of each other, having been separated into different care homes. A friend said, "Sidney and Edith were fine before. Doctors can say what they like, but I know that they died of broken hearts."

I read it twice. And I said, "It's just like
Joe and the New Rabbit."

On the way home from school, me and
Suzanne and Tom went to get some of Miss
Matheson's tall parsley from the shed. The
smell wafted out when we opened the door.

We took a piece down to the New Rabbit.
It looked even worse than ever.

Suzanne said, "What if the New Rabbit
dies?" We went back to the shed.

Suzanne got the newspaper page out of
her pocket and pinned it on the wall next to
the map to Joe's Dad's apartment and the
list of things Joe didn't like about living at
his Dad's.

"What are we going to do?" I asked.

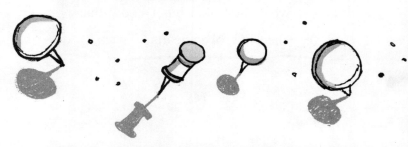

Suzanne said, "We have to get Joe and his rabbit back together."

We started making a plan.

ANNA'S AND TOM'S AND SUZANNE'S PLANS TO GET JOE-DOWN-THE-STREET AND THE NEW RABBIT BACK TOGETHER AND RESCUE THEM BEFORE THEY BOTH DIE

PLAN NUMBER 1
Tell Mom that Joe and his rabbit are going to die and ask her to go and rescue Joe

PLAN NUMBER 2
Get Joe's Dad's phone number and phone Joe and tell him that his rabbit and him are going to die if he doesn't come home

PLAN NUMBER 3

Write Joe's Dad a letter pretending to be the landlord and tell him that the rules have changed from "NO PETS" to "NO PETS EXCEPT RABBITS"

PLAN NUMBER 4

Go and rescue Joe ourselves

There was a knock on the shed door.

"What's the password?" I said.

Mom said, "Trouble. Your dinner is ready. And Suzanne's Dad's been on the phone."

So we pinned the plan on the wall, and Suzanne took the Rabbit Monitor because it was her turn, and we came out of the shed, and I locked the padlock.

And Mom said, "What is that awful smell?"

And Suzanne said, "Tom," even though it was really Miss Matheson's parsley.

And Mom said, "Tom, that's a big smell for a small person. Maybe you should go to the toilet."

And me and Tom went inside. And Suzanne went home. And we heard Suzanne's Dad shouting through the wall about what time it was, and where she'd been, and coming straight home from school and all that.

After dinner, when Mom was watching *Coronation Street*, I said, "Mom . . ."

And Mom said, "Yes . . ."

"Can you drive to Joe-down-the-street's

Dad's apartment and rescue Joe, please?"

And Mom said, "Mmm?"

And then she said, "No."

And Tom said, "Why?"

"Because it's a school night."

And I said, "Please."

And Mom said, "No."

And Tom said, "Why?"

"Because."

And Tom said, "If you don't, Joe's New Rabbit and Joe will die."

And Mom said, "Joe's Rabbit is fine. And so is Joe. No one needs to be rescued!"

And I said, "What's Joe's Dad's phone number?"

And Mom said, "Why?"

And I said, "Because."

And Mom said, "Are you going to tell Joe this rubbish about his rabbit dying?"

"No."

Mom gave me Joe's
number. I dialed it. Mom
was still standing in the room, so
I said, "Did you want something?"
Because that's what Mom always says
to me when I hang around when *she's*
on the phone.

Mom said, "*Watch* it, Anna," and went
away.

Joe's Dad answered.

"Is Joe there?"

And he put Joe on.

"Hello, Joe."

I heard Mom pick up the other phone
upstairs. Mom doesn't know that you have to
hold the quiet button down if you don't want
the other person to know you're listening in.

So I couldn't say anything about the New

QUIET

Rabbit and how me and Suzanne had found out that Joe and the New Rabbit were probably going to die.

So I just said, "Can you tell me your address, please, because me and Suzanne want to send you a birthday card."

And Joe said, "It isn't my birthday until August."

And I said, "So?"

"That's in four months."

I said, "We have to make it first."

"Oh."

Joe told me the address, and I wrote it down.

And then he said, "Is the New Rabbit okay?"

And I was going to say, "No," but I heard Mom say, "Ahem" on the other phone, so I said, "Yes. It's fine."

And then I said, "How are *you*?"

And Joe said, "Itchy. My eczema's back."

And I said, "Okay, then. Bye." And I put the phone down.

Mom came down and said, "Why do you want Joe's address?"

And I said, "Were you listening in?" Because that's what Mom always says to me.

And Mom said, "*Anna* . . ."

And I said, "I'm going to see Suzanne."

And Mom said, "No. You're not. You're going to do your homework, and read your book, and then it's time for bed."

I went into my bedroom and I got the walkie-talkie. "Anna to Suzanne. Anna to Suzanne. Come in, Suzanne. Over."

"Suzanne to Anna. Suzanne to Anna. Receiving you loud and clear. Over."

"I have tried Plan One." (Which was the one about getting Mom to drive to Joe's house to rescue him.) "But Mom says she won't rescue Joe. And I have tried to do Plan Two." (Which is the one where we phone Joe to tell him to come home.) "But I couldn't talk to Joe about it because Mom was listening in and she said I wasn't allowed to say anything to Joe about his rabbit. Over."

"Copy that. We will have to try Plan Three. Over."

Which was the one where we write a letter to Joe's Dad from the landlord.

I was going to tell Suzanne about how Joe had said that his eczema had come back again, but I didn't get a chance to say anything else because Mom came in and

she took the walkie-talkie off me and she said, "Homework!"

And I heard Suzanne saying, "Anna? Anna? Are you receiving me? Over."

CHAPTER 15
"Rabbits Don't Scream"

In the morning we went and looked in on the New Rabbit again and took it some more of the tall smelly parsley from the shed. The rabbit looked even worse than before. On the way to school, Suzanne said that she had had a dream in the night, and in her dream the rabbit was screaming.

I said, "I don't think rabbits scream."

And Suzanne said, "In my dream it did."

After school Suzanne brought all her pens

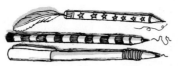

to the shed. We decided that Suzanne should write the letter because she has got the best handwriting. And I said what she should write down. We had to do a lot of practice letters, because for one thing Suzanne isn't very good at spelling and she kept putting the words all wrong. And for another thing, I kept changing my mind about what the words should be, like whether it should say "from" or "love from" or "yours sincerely."

Anyway, in the end we put . . .

Dear Mr. Walker (Joe's Dad),

I have changed the rules about pets from NO PETS to NO PETS EXCEPT RABBITS. If you see me, do not ask me about rabbits, though, please, because I don't want to talk about it.

Yours sincerely,

The Landlord

P.S. Please do not let the rabbit go on the stairs or in the elevator, because I do not want poos and rabbit fluff getting trod into the carpet.

We put the letter in an envelope, and Suzanne wrote the address on it, and I put a stamp on and licked the envelope shut, and we took it to the post box at the bottom of the road, and we lifted Tom up to post it, because posting letters is one of Tom's favorite things.

And Suzanne said she couldn't stop thinking about her dream with the rabbit screaming.

So we went home, and we put "rabbit screaming" in the computer, and this is what it said . . .

"A rabbit scream is a shrill sound, not unlike the scream of a small child. It generally signifies the rabbit is dying."

❧ CHAPTER 16 ☙
A Real-Life Rescue

I was in bed when I heard it. It woke me up.

Mom came into my room. "Anna, what's the matter?" She felt me on the forehead. "You screamed," she said. "Did you have a bad dream?"

I said that I had.

Mom stroked me on the head. And I lay back down and pretended to fall asleep until she went back to bed.

Because it wasn't *me* who had screamed.

It had come from under my bed. Where the Rabbit Monitor was.

I got my walkie-talkie and I whispered, "Suzanne, are you asleep?"

Suzanne didn't speak.

"Suzanne, are you there?" I went under the covers. **"SUZANNE, THE RABBIT SCREAMED!"**

The walkie-talkie crackled. "Copy that," Suzanne said. "Meet me at the shed. Over and out."

I got out of bed and felt my way, in the dark, through my bedroom door and along the wall in the corridor, until I came to the top of the stairs. I'm not scared of the dark, because I'm nine, but some things in our house aren't nice at night, when the lights aren't on. Like the photo of Dad's Great-Grandma with the black lace veil on her face, and the spider plant with the tentacles

that touch you when you go past, and the post with the coats on it at the bottom of the stairs that sometimes looks like a person.

And this time the stair post looked *a lot* like a person. And as I got near it, I saw one of the arms was reaching out. And when I got to the bottom, I thought it tried to touch me.

I ran past it, into the kitchen, to the back door, and turned the handle fast. And then I felt something behind me, tapping me on the back. I froze.

"Are you going out?"

"Tom?"

"Yes?"

"Oh." I turned around. He was in his Batman pajamas and his Bob the Builder hard hat.

"I thought you were something else."

"No," Tom said. "Where are you going?"

"To the shed."

"I'll come."

And I said that he could, because, for one thing, he was already putting his wellies on, and for another thing, I didn't want him getting the Screaming Habdabs and waking up Mom, and for an even other thing, I was glad it was him who had tapped me on the back, and not a coat that had got down off the stair post on its own, or anything like that.

It was cold outside, and the moon was out, and the stars. The sky was big. And when I looked up, it made me feel a bit sick. It was quiet. I held my nose and popped my ears, to hear clearer.

Tom turned on the light on his Bob the Builder hard hat. The light shone on Suzanne. She was waiting by the shed.

"Follow me," she said.

The back lane looked different in the dark.

"Come on, Tom," I said, and I told him it was best to look straight ahead, not out to the sides, where the bushes are, because in the dark you can sometimes see things that aren't really there. And I said that if he wanted, he could hold on to my hand. But Tom said he was Batman, and Bob the Builder, so he wasn't scared.

When we got to the bottom of the lane, I looked up at Joe's house. It was so dark, you couldn't see the windows, or the door, only the shape of the outside. Like the houses Mrs. Peters cut out of black card, to put at the back of the stage when we did the school play.

Suzanne opened the gate.

We crouched down by the hutch. I opened the latch and pushed back some of the hay. The New Rabbit was on its side. There was dribble round its mouth. And its eyes were all strange.

"Is it dead?" Tom said.

The New Rabbit groaned, and twitched its feet.

"Not yet," said Suzanne.

"What are we going to do?" I asked.

Suzanne said we should go back to the shed and make a plan.

I was glad to get away from the New Rabbit, and to be inside the shed with the worms and the wood lice and the wasp trap and all

that. I closed the door. We looked at the plans pinned up on the wall.

"We've tried Plan Number One, and Number Two, and Number Three," Suzanne said.

There was only one plan left. It was Plan Number Four: Rescue Joe Ourselves. I looked at the map to his Dad's apartment that Joe had drawn. It was a long way away. Past the Bottom Bus Stop, and over the bridge, and round the roundabout, and down the track, and through the old tunnel, and through the gate, and across the field. All in the dark.

"Joe's Dad might come and collect the New Rabbit in the morning when he reads our letter from the landlord," I said. "And if he doesn't, we could rescue Joe tomorrow, straight after school."

"Tomorrow might be too late," Suzanne

said. "We need to go tonight."

"How are we going to get there?" I asked.

"We'll walk," said Suzanne.

I said I didn't think walking was a good idea.

"How else?" Suzanne said.

"Erm . . . bus?"

Suzanne made her eyebrows go up, and said, "*Anna*," the way I hate. "You don't get buses in the middle of the *night*."

And I said how you did, actually, and that's why it's called a night bus.

Suzanne said she had never heard of a night bus, and there was, "no such thing."

And I said that just because she didn't know about it didn't mean it didn't exist. Because there were millions of things in the world that Suzanne had never heard of. And I tried to think of one, which was

hard because Suzanne has actually heard of most things, and because Tom kept pulling at my pajamas and saying, "Anna . . . Anna . . . ANNA . . ."

So I stopped trying to think, and said, **"WHAT?!"**

"Look." Tom was pointing to something shiny at the back of the shed, near the floor, underneath an old sheet. The light from his Bob the Builder hard hat was making it glint.

I went closer. It was a reflector, on the spoke of a bicycle wheel. I pulled away the old sheet. *"The Super-Speed-Bike-Machine!"*

Me and Suzanne checked the training wheels, and the tires, and the lights. And Tom rang the bell and made the wheels spin round, and all the reflectors shone, and the spokies went up and down.

And Suzanne said we should write a list
of things we needed.

So we did. This is what it said . . .

ANNA'S AND SUZANNE'S AND TOM'S LIST OF THINGS WE NEED TO RESCUE JOE-DOWN-THE-STREET

The Super-Speed-Bike-Machine

Tom's Bob the Builder hard hat with the
light turned on

Walkie-talkies

2 flashlights (one for Anna, one for Suzanne)

A whistle

A compass

Cookies

Life jacket

Snorkel

Camouflage

When the list was finished, Suzanne said we had too many things, and they would take too long to find. So we crossed the compass off because, like she said, we didn't know whether Joe's house was north or south or anything anyway. And we crossed off the life jacket, and the snorkel, and the whistle as well. And Suzanne wanted to cross off the cookies, too, but Tom said if we weren't taking cookies he was staying at home, so I sneaked back into the house to get some. And I got two flashlights as well, one for me and one for Suzanne. And then we went into the garden and smeared camouflage mud on our faces from Miss Matheson's flower bed.

We got the Super-Speed-Bike-Machine out of the shed. And we walked it down the back lane. And Suzanne said we should have one last look at the New Rabbit, just in case. Because, like she said, there wasn't much point in going to rescue Joe, to bring him back to his rabbit, if it was already dead.

Suzanne shone her light into the hutch. The New Rabbit opened its eyes and groaned. I said maybe we should take the New Rabbit with us, in case it died while we were gone. And Suzanne said that was a good idea.

So I picked the New Rabbit up, and I wrapped Suzanne's coat around it. And I passed it to Tom, in the trailer, to hold. The New Rabbit closed its eyes. Tom

held it close, and stroked it behind the ears, and spoke to it nice and low.

And then Suzanne said, "Shh . . ." because she had heard something.

I listened. There was a jingling sound. I saw two yellow eyes, in the dark, up the road. "It's the Cat Attack Alarm!" I said.

"Quick," said Suzanne. "Let's go."

I got on the saddle of the Super-Speed-Bike-Machine, and Suzanne got on the stunt pegs. And the New Cat came nearer. And when it saw the New Rabbit, it stared, and got down low, and its eyes went very wide.

Suzanne looked at the map. "Turn left!" she said.

I turned on the light. Tom held on tight, and Suzanne pushed off, and I started to pedal as fast as I could, and we all said,

"THREE, TWO, ONE, BLAST OFF!"

And we went off, flying, down the hill, right in the middle of the road, because we were the only ones out. And we whizzed past the horse trough where Tom wets his wellies, and the shops, and the Bottom Bus Stop.

And Suzanne said, **"NOW WE'RE OUT-OF-BOUNDS!"**

And I rang the bell, and the wind made my eyes water, and Tom did the Batman song in the trailer in the back. And me and Suzanne got The Hysterics.

And when we came to the bridge, Suzanne said, "Stop!" and she put her foot out, and I slammed on the brakes, because the traffic lights were on red.

We waited until the light went green. And we rode over the bridge. It was so quiet, we could hear the river underneath. When we

got to the roundabout, Suzanne said, "Go left."

And I did. Well, I *thought* I did, but I'm not very good with my left and my right. And roundabouts are hard.

"That's *right*," Suzanne said. "Not right, *left*!"

"Left?"

"Right, yes!"

"Make up your mind!"

In the end we went round it about a million times. And Tom said he felt sick, and Suzanne told him to stop eating all the cookies. And then she said, "Anna, *here*!" And she grabbed the handlebars, and the Super-Speed-Bike-Machine turned, and we came off the roundabout,

and hit a bit of gravel, and skidded, and the trailer hit a bump, and Tom and the New Rabbit and the trailer went flying, up in the air, and the trailer and Tom came down again with a thump.

And Tom said, "Ouch."

But he wasn't hurt because he said he was, "saved by my Bob the Builder hard hat!"

"Where's the New Rabbit?" I said.

Tom looked down at his hands. It was gone.

Me and Suzanne got the walkie-talkies out. We stood back-to-back. And Suzanne walked one way, and I walked the other, and we shone our flashlights from side to side.

"Suzanne to Anna. Suzanne to Anna. Come in, Anna. I'm at the gorse bush. What's your position? Over."

"Anna to Suzanne. Anna to Suzanne. I'm at the traffic cone. Over."

"Copy that. Traffic cone. Are you receiving me? Over."

"Yes."

Suzanne said, "You're supposed to say, 'Receiving you loud and clear.'"

And I said, "We haven't got time to do all the 'Come ins,' and the 'Copies,' and the 'Over and outs' and all that. Let's just look for the New Rabbit!"

And then Suzanne started going on about her Uncle again, and how he's in the army. And about how I shouldn't have wrapped the New Rabbit in her coat because she was cold, and if it was lost, she would be in Big Trouble with her Dad.

And I said how losing someone's coat wasn't as bad as losing someone's rabbit, and what were we going to say to Joe-down-the-street? And then I saw something.

"Look. In the river!" I shone my light on the water.

Me and Suzanne and Tom stood on the bank. Suzanne's coat floated past.

"Can rabbits swim?" Tom asked.

And me and Suzanne didn't answer, because we both knew that they can't. And that the New Rabbit must have drowned. And Tom started to cry.

And I told him he was Batman and Bob the Builder, to try to make him stop. But he didn't. And he took his hard hat off, and put it on the ground.

And then Suzanne said, "Shh, listen." There was a jingling sound. It was coming from the bridge. There were two yellow

eyes, in the dark, on the wall. "It's the Cat Attack Alarm again."

The New Cat came close, and it got down very low, and its eyes went very wide, and it stared at something near the edge of the river. And then it disappeared down the bank. And when it came back up, it was dragging something in its mouth. It dropped something white next to Tom's feet. I shone my flashlight on it. The white thing opened its eyes. They were pink.

"The New Rabbit!" Tom said. And he stopped crying and stroked the New Cat on its head until its ears went flat. And he gave it a cookie. Which the New Cat didn't really like. And then the New Cat went back off over the bridge.

Tom got back in the trailer with the New Rabbit, and I sat on the saddle, and Suzanne stood on the stunt pegs. And Suzanne pushed off and I started to pedal. And we carried on down the track, on the Super-Speed-Bike-Machine, until we came to the old tunnel.

We went inside.

It was so dark in the tunnel, even with the flashlights, that we couldn't see the sides.

Suzanne shouted, "Hello . . ."

It echoed back, "Hello . . . *low* . . . *low* . . ."

"Is there anybody there?" Suzanne said.

And the echo said, "There . . . *ere* . . . *ere* . . ."

And we called out our names, and they echoed back, until we came out on the other side.

Suzanne looked at the map. "We have to go through the gate and across the field."

202

We got off the Super-Speed-Bike-Machine and hid it in the bushes.

Tom wasn't sure about going into the field because when we got near, we could see there were cows. And Tom doesn't like cows because he says they're too big. But I told Tom how cows never hurt anyone. And in the end Tom said okay.

We opened the big gate. And Suzanne held the rabbit. And then we closed it again. Like the sign on it said.

And the cows turned to look at us, and one of them said, **"Mooo . . . ,"** but they didn't move.

The field was full of cowpats, and it was so muddy, it was hard to get across. And Tom's wellies kept getting stuck.

When we got to the other side, there were some buildings straight ahead. We looked at the picture that Joe had done. It matched. We counted the windows along to where Joe's bedroom was. And we threw stones up at it.

A light came on, and the curtains went back, and we saw Joe's face. The window opened.

I said, "Hello, Joe."

And Joe said, "Who's that?"

Because it probably didn't look very like me because of the dark, and the cowpats, and the camouflage on my face and all that.

And I said, "It's Anna."

And Suzanne said, "And Suzanne."

And Tom said, "And Tom."

"We've come to rescue you," said Suzanne.

Joe closed his window. And his curtains. And at first we thought he had gone back to bed. But then a door opened, downstairs.

Joe came out. And we told him all about how the New Rabbit had got poorly again, after he'd gone. And about the old couple in the paper, who got separated and died of broken hearts. And about Suzanne's dream. And how the New Rabbit had screamed.

And Joe held the New Rabbit very close, and he put it inside his pajama top, and he kissed it all over its face. And he said, "Let's go home."

And me and Tom and Suzanne and Joe started back across the field. Which Tom said he didn't mind this time because the cows had gone.

Until we got to the middle, when one appeared, right in front of us, in the dark.

"Mooo . . . ," it said.

We stopped. The cow stared. And then another cow came, and another, and another.

I told Tom to ignore them.

Because of how cows had never hurt anyone.

And I said, "Isn't that right, Joe?" Because Joe always knows about things.

And Joe said how that wasn't *exactly* right, because cows had hurt some people, and once it was someone who was walking his dog, and it was definitely true because it was on the news, and he was called Chris Poole.

And I said how they probably didn't hurt him very badly, and it was probably only by mistake.

And Joe said how they had kicked him, and broken his ribs, and he was only saved because he was in the police and his friend

rescued him in his helicopter. And if he hadn't, the cows would have trampled him to death.

"Oh," I said.

The cows came around us in a circle. And they rolled their eyes and licked their lips. And I heard something roar, and at first I thought it was the noise cows make just

before they trample you. So I closed my eyes.

But then I heard it again, and this time it sounded more like a car. So I opened my eyes. And I saw two headlights. And I heard a car horn. And I heard, "Spot on, Skipper. Four sprogs. And they're surrounded. Got 'em in the old illuminators. Fall out."

It was Mr. Tucker. In his old sports car, wearing his driving goggles and his gloves. And Mrs. Rotherham was with him.

Mrs. Rotherham got out of the car, and she opened the gate, and then she got back in, and Mr. Tucker drove the car right into the field, and he flashed the lights and honked the horn. And Mrs. Rotherham waved her walking stick. And the cows all scattered.

And Mr. Tucker stopped the car and he said, "Hallo, Basher." And he gave Tom the salute.

And Tom gave Mr. Tucker the salute back.

And Mr. Tucker said, "Hop in!"

And Tom got on Mr. Tucker's knee, and Mr. Tucker said, "Bit of cowpat in the cockpit there, Basher."

And the rest of us piled in the back.

And Mr. Tucker said, "Good God. Overload."

And he put his goggles over his eyes and tightened his driving gloves and he said,

"Honk, honk!" Like Toad of Toad Hall does in my *Wind in the Willows* book at home.

And Mr. Tucker drove us home even faster than the Super-Speed-Bike-Machine.

﹡ CHAPTER 17 ﹡
The Poisoned Parsley

That was just about everything that happened in the Great Rabbit Rescue.

When we got home, there were two police cars outside. Mom and Dad, and Suzanne's Mom and Dad, and Joe's Mom, and two policemen were in our kitchen.

I thought we were in Big Trouble then, but nobody shouted, not even Suzanne's Dad.

And Mom cuddled me and Tom in.

And Suzanne and her Mom and Dad went to their house.

And Joe and his Mom and the New Rabbit went to their house.

And the policemen filled in their forms. And they went home as well.

And Mom made some tea for Mrs. Rotherham. And Mr. Tucker said he'd prefer something stronger. And Dad brought him some brandy. And Mr. Tucker said, "That's the ticket. Just a snifter." And he drank it down in one.

And Mom made some hot milk for me and Tom. And Tom fell asleep on Mr. Tucker's knee before his milk even came. And Mr. Tucker fell asleep too.

And he started snoring. And Mom and Mrs. Rotherham got The Hysterics.

And then Mrs. Rotherham told Mom the story of how her and Mr. Tucker found us. And how she had seen the police cars, and come down the road, and how Mr. Tucker was out, asking the police what was going on. And how the policemen said we were missing. And how Mrs. Rotherham had seen the tire tracks from the Super-Speed-Bike-Machine at the bottom of the road, and that the hutch was open, and that the New Rabbit was gone, and how she went up to the shed and saw all Joe's pictures about his rabbit, and the list about what he didn't like about living at his Dad's, and our plans on the wall, and how they had all been ticked off, except number four, which was, "Rescue Joe Ourselves."

And how she found the piece of paper

213

with Joe's Dad's address. And how her and Mr. Tucker tried to tell the police, but they said they had to take statements from everyone first. And how Mr. Tucker said, "Humph, Old Gendarmerie, load of old bull and bumph." And got his old sports car out of the garage.

And that's all I remember, because then I fell asleep as well.

The next day me and Suzanne and Tom and Joe stayed home from school. And Joe came round in the morning to tell us that his Mom had taken the New Rabbit to the vet, and how the vet had given the New Rabbit some pills and said that the New Rabbit wasn't dying of a broken heart at all. It was dying because it had been poisoned.

And Suzanne said we had better do an investigation to find out who had poisoned it.

So we went to see Mrs. Rotherham to ask her to help us, because of how she used to be in the police and everything.

And Suzanne said, "Who could have done it?"

And Mrs. Rotherham said, "Who *indeed*?"

Digitalis
Foxglove

And she gave me and Suzanne a file with a label on it that said, "The Case of the Poisoned Rabbit." And inside it was our Spy Club notebook, which Mrs. Rotherham had taken from the shed. And she had highlighted the bits about Joe going away, and about us feeding the New Rabbit, and the New Rabbit being unwell. And there were some privet leaves, and daffodils, and apple seeds, and some of the strange-smelling parsley from

Hedera helix
English
Common Ivy

Miss Matheson's garden in the
file as well. All in see-through
plastic bags, sealed up. And
they had tags on them that
said, "*Evidence.*" And there
was an old book with pictures
of poisonous flowers and plants, and
one of the corners of the pages was
folded down. And on the page it said,
"Common house and garden plants
toxic to leporid creatures." And all of the
things in the little bags inside the file were
on the list. And at the bottom
of the list it said, "*Aethusa
cynapium*, or fool's or

Aethusa Cynapium
Fool's PARSLEY

poison parsley, easily distinguished from parsley proper by its height, girth, and foul-smelling odor."

Me and Suzanne looked up "leporid" in my dictionary. It said . . .

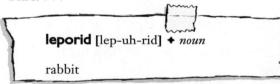

leporid [lep-uh-rid] ✦ *noun*
an animal of the family Leporidae,
comprising the rabbits and hares

And we looked in Suzanne's as well. It said . . .

leporid [lep-uh-rid] ✦ *noun*
rabbit

The next day, at school, Joe sat back in his old seat. And Mrs. Peters called Joe's name out last, taking roll. And Joe said, "Here."

Mrs. Rotherham didn't tell anyone what had really happened with Joe-down-the-street

and his rabbit and why it nearly died. And neither did me and Suzanne.

But we took the rest of the parsley out of the shed. And we put it on Miss Matheson's compost heap. And we hid the file of the Case of the Poisoned Rabbit next to the Spy Club notebook, behind the worms and the wasp trap, on the shelf in the shed.

Me and Suzanne don't go on the walkie-talkies as much anymore. Not now that Joe is back down the road. Because mostly we play Dingo the Dog, and Mountain Rescue, and see how long we can stare at the sun before we go blind and all that.

We aren't allowed back on the Super-Speed-Bike-Machine, though. Dad took me and Tom to find it, in the bushes, by the field by Joe's house. And when we got it home, and Mom saw how the training wheels were hanging off, and the back wheel was bent, and one of the tires had burst, she said, "That contraption is condemned."

And she tried to put it out with the trash cans.

But me and Tom begged, and in the end she let us put it back in the shed. Under the dust sheet, behind the stepladders, and the plant stakes and the broken old floorboards.

Suzanne says that when we're older, and we haven't got any bounds to be in, we can take the walkie-talkies as far away as we want. And one of us can go on the Super-Speed-Bike-Machine, and the other one can go on buses and boats and things like that.

And then Suzanne says she will say, "Suzanne to Anna. Suzanne to Anna. I'm in America. Are you receiving me? Over."

And I will say, "Anna to Suzanne. Anna to

Suzanne. I'm in Afghanistan. Receiving you loud and clear. Over."

Because those places are about the same far apartness from here. We've measured it on a map.

And when we do it, I'm going to get Tom to come with me, and Suzanne is going to take Joe-down-the-street.

Because Tom and Joe love the Super-Speed-Bike-Machine, and buses, and boats and things like that. And they don't like being left behind.

The End

tHE knACker's ABC
(L'eQUarRissAge PoUR tOUs)
pLAy by BOriS ViaN

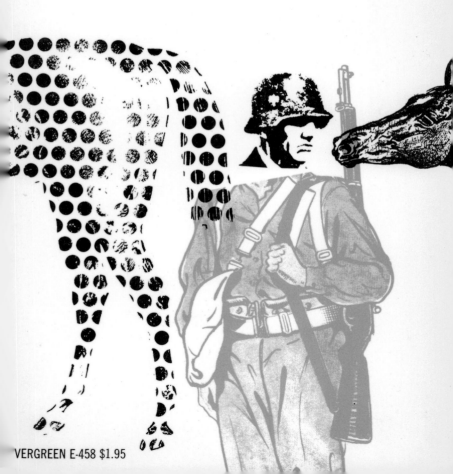

VERGREEN E-458 $1.95

The Knacker's
ABC

Previously Published

The Empire Builders
The Generals' Tea Party

The Knacker's ABC

(L' Equarrissage pour tous)

*A paramilitary vaudeville
in one long act*

by Boris Vian

Translated by
Simon Watson Taylor

Grove Press, Inc.
New York

Originally published as *L'Equarrissage pour tous* by Editions Toutain, Paris, 1950. Second edition in Boris Vian's *Théâtre* published by Editions Jean-Jacques Pauvert, Paris, copyright © 1965 by Jean-Jacques Pauvert.

Library of Congress Catalog Card Number: 68:17721

First Printing

Manufactured in the United States of America

to my close enemy:
CHARLEMAGNE

Greetings to Boris Vian
from
Jean Cocteau

With *L'Equarrissage pour tous* (*The Knacker's ABC*), Boris Vian has just given us an astonishing play which stands as solitary in its own troubled era as did Apollinaire's *Mamelles de Tirésias* (*Breasts of Tiresias*) in his own and my *Mariés de la Tour Eiffel* (*Young Married Couple of the Eiffel Tower*) in mine.

This play, or vocal ballet, possesses an exquisite insolence, light and heavy by turn, comparable to the syncopated rhythms of which Boris Vian is the master.

Suddenly we are in the center of time, at that precise moment when time ceases to exist, when acts lose their meaning in the motionless heart of the cyclone, in that place where the present and the future are knotted like a piece of old discarded string.

And laughter explodes when the bomb explodes, and the bomb explodes with laughter, and the respect one shows toward catastrophes explodes, too, like a soap bubble.

A group of merry young actors, busy in the wings transforming themselves into Germans, Americans, Resistance Fighters, paratroopers, gallop across the stage, fall from the flies, leap up staircases leading nowhere, bump up against each other, mingle and then detach themselves in a void which is full to the brim.

Nothing could be more serious than this farce which is not a farce and yet is one, reflecting what we are compelled to take seriously and which is really only serious

7

in two respects: the death of our fellow men and the certainty that this somber farce comes to an end only because of physical exhaustion—and then only for the short rest necessary for the participants to get their breath back and start over again as quickly as possible.

Yes, this is what a man with the inspired gift of playing the trumpet or rather of giving the shape of a trumpet to his inspiration, this, I say, is what a man with rhythm in his soul has hurled in our faces like a bouquet in a battle of stinking flowers.

A salutory undertaking, and excellent propaganda for the rest of us timid people, limited as we are to confronting the plural with the singular and to staying free in a world where freedom is desperately sick and in full flight.

Preface

L'Equarrissage pour tous, written at the beginning of 1946, had to wait four years for its first performance. I was surprised to see this play frequently meet with a timid reception from a number of producers noted for their imaginative outlook. To mention only two, Grenier and Hussenot hesitated two years before deciding . . . not to put it on. Jean-Louis Barrault had it in his hands in July 1949 and was supposed to stage it in October 1949. But he never did. Getting rather impatient at seeing the actuality of the satirical element in this entertainment diminishing as the days went by, I asked him to let me have the script back so that I could show it to André Reybaz, who had already been told about the play by Barrault himself at the time when Reybaz's Compagnie du Myrmidon was staging *Fastes d'Enfer* at the Marigny. Briefly, Reybaz and his comrades pulled the Knacker's household together in two weeks of frantic rehearsal and pushed them on to the stage of the Noctambules. I must make it clear that the members of the audience never misunderstood my intentions: all those who came to see the play enjoyed themselves and only started having mental reservations afterward. What annoys me is that the critics seem to regard laughter as a rather degrading activity unless it is directed at falling pants and deceived husbands. I am bold enough to consider that one can try to make people laugh by other means and that there is nothing scandalous in provoking hilarity by evoking war, for example. I must confess to being among those in whom war inspires neither patriotic reflexes, nor a pugnacious out-jutting of the chin, nor murderous enthusiasm

(Rosalie! Rosalie! queen of the bayonet!), nor poignant and emotional good-fellowship, nor sudden piety—nothing but a desperate, all-consuming anger against the absurdity of battles which are battles of words but which kill men of flesh and blood. An impotent anger, unfortunately. Among other possibilities, there is one means of escape: raillery. I have been accused of seeking scandal with *L'Equar-rissage pour tous*: nothing could be further from the truth. I can assure my critics that I am not afraid of scandal and if I were seeking it I would do so more shrewdly and more effectively. This accusation has been hurled at me chiefly because it is more convenient to catalogue someone than to take the trouble to listen to what he has to say (this is not a reproach, on the contrary; those who catalogue me save me, in my turn, the trouble of reading their remarks, since they simply repeat their parrot-phrases each time they set pen to paper).

Besides, I explained some of my intentions in an article written for *Opéra* which appeared on April 12, 1950—I quote myself not for pleasure but simply because it does not seem to me necessary to rephrase something which still represents my viewpoint exactly:

> War, that grotesque obscenity, has the peculiarity (among others) of being invasive and importunate, and those who are amused by it usually consider themselves justified in extending it to those who are not amused by it. It is the most destructive of the multiple images of intolerance. Which is why I have tried to take action against it to the limited extent to which anything written and artificial can be effective; the concept of fighting war by means of war, as some choose to do, seems to be quite intolerable, and there

remains, alas, only a limited choice of alternative methods.

However, I hope that all these intentions are not too apparent. The play is above all a burlesque: it seemed to me that the best approach to war was to laugh at its expense, a craftier but more effective way of fighting it (though to hell with efficacity anyway). Enough. If I go on like this, people will think I have written something in the nature of "propaganda for men of good will," a thought that makes me shudder with horror.

The story? The whole action takes place on June 6, 1944, at Arromanches. Apparently an important event is taking place that day: the Anglo-American forces are landing to crush the Germans occupying France. But this event is of secondary importance for the hero of the play, the father, whose own problem is to decide whether or not he should marry off his daughter to the German who has been sharing her bed for four years.

The play gradually unfolds the solution which presents itself to this problem. The atmosphere is provided by the temporary elements: soldiers of various nationalities, Resistance Fighters, gunfire, and destruction. The stable element consists of the daughter and her marriage. There is no moral to the story: in fact it has an unhappy ending—war is the final victor.

It only remains for me to thank Jean Cocteau for the article he was kind enough to write for *Opéra* (May 3, 1950). I ask him to regard these few lines as a mark of my gratitude and friendship.

Finally, I should add that without André Reybaz, Catherine Toth, and their talented and disinterested company,

I should have abandoned all hope of ever seeing *L'Equarrissage pour tous* staged, which is a measure of my indebtedness to them.

BORIS VIAN

Paris, 1950

L'Equarrissage pour tous was first performed by the Compagnie du Myrmidon at the Théâtre des Noctambules, Paris, on April 16, 1950, in a production directed by André Reybaz, designed by Yves Faucher, and with the following cast:

THE FATHER, *a horse knacker*	André Reybaz
ANDRE, *an apprentice knacker*	Paul Crauchet
THE NEIGHBOR	Guy Saint-Jean
FIRST GERMAN SOLDIER	Michel Calonne
FIRST AMERICAN SOLDIER	Jean-Pierre Hebrard
MARIE	Catherine Toth
THE MOTHER	Yette Lucas
SECOND GERMAN SOLDIER	Jean Mauvais
SECOND AMERICAN SOLDIER	Roger Paschel
POSTMISTRESS	Odette Piquet
TWO AMERICAN SOLDIERS (*chorus*)	René Lafforgue
	Jean-Pierre Hebrard
TWO GERMAN SOLDIERS (*chorus*)	Jean Mauvais
	Michel Calonne
HEINZ SCHNITTERMACH	Jacques Muller
A NONDESCRIPT SOLDIER	*
MARIE-CYPRIENNE	Nicole Jonesco
JACQUES	Jacques Verrières
JAPANESE PARATROOPER	Jacques Muller
CATHERINE	Zanie Campan
VINCENT, *a big French Resistance leader*	René Lafforgue
COLONEL LORIOT, *a little French Resistance leader*	Jacques Muller
TWO SISTERS OF CHARITY	Odette Piquet
	Roger Paschel
CAPTAIN KÜNSTERLICH	Jean Mauvais

AN AMERICAN ARMY CHAPLAIN   Roger Paschel

FOUR MEMBERS OF THE SALVATION ARMY
    (*the American-German chorus transformed*)

FRENCH ARMY CAPTAIN   Jean Mauvais

FRENCH ARMY LIEUTENANT   René Lafforgue

THREE ARMY SAPPERS   *

---

* The NONDESCRIPT SOLDIER does not appear in the original cast list. The THREE ARMY SAPPERS were replaced by a BOY SCOUT, played by Yves Faucher--see Translator's Note at end of play.

The action takes place on June 6, 1944, during the morning, in the home of a most amiable knacker. The setting of the play is the living room of the knacker's house in Arromanches, where the Normandy landing is taking place at this very moment. Workbench and tool chest in one corner. Tables, chairs. Doors leading wherever necessary for exits and entrances. A large painting of a horse's head on one wall. A knacker's pit under the floor, equipped with trap door worked by a lever. Odor sui generis. General atmosphere bucolic or, to be more precise, Arromanchian. As the curtain rises the FATHER *and his son* ANDRE *are at the workbench trying to reassemble an enormous jack plane.*

FATHER: That's done it! That last bloody horse has just about ruined this plane.

ANDRE: As bad as that?

FATHER: Just look at the blade! . . . Screwed up good and proper! . . .

ANDRE: Maybe it will still work . . .

FATHER: It'll damn well have to.

He takes the blade, glares at it and spits on it disgustedly. ANDRE *hands him a rag with which the* FATHER *wipes off the spit. Outside, various noises: machine-gun fire, explosions, etc. . . . Cries, shouts and oaths of military pungency.*

FATHER: This landing of theirs! It's beginning to get my goat. We should have had our heads examined, coming to live in Arromanches!

15

ANDRE: You're darn right!

FATHER: Hey, you! A little respect for my great-grand-father: it was his idea.

ANDRE: Sorry. I'll try to remember.

FATHER: Where's my daughter?

ANDRE: Which one?

FATHER: Marie.

ANDRE: They're both called Marie.

FATHER: Ah yes, so they are! . . . Oh well, forget it.

ANDRE: I'll go and look for her. (*He leaves the room.*)

FATHER (*alone*): Alone, huh? A quick nip while nobody's looking! (*He tiptoes stealthily up to the wall cupboard where the Calvados is kept, and reaches for it. Just as he gets his hands on the bottle a violent explosion shakes the room. Things fall off the mantelpiece and walls. He gives a jump.*) Christ almighty! The lousy sods! . . .

Violent knocking on the door.

Come in!

Enter the NEIGHBOR.

NEIGHBOR: Hi!

FATHER: Hi! Still alive, eh?

NEIGHBOR: You too, eh?

FATHER: Don't worry about me! I'm a knacker. They'll never come near my house. The stink's too horrible.

NEIGHBOR: You're not kidding. It's the worst stink I've ever come across. How do you manage to produce such a rotten stink?

FATHER: It's a family secret. Here, I'll whisper it in your ear.

NEIGHBOR: You've already told me a hundred times.

FATHER (*annoyed*): Well, you just asked me.

NEIGHBOR: Out of politeness. I'm not a complete idiot, you know.

FATHER: What about this military landing? How's it going?

NEIGHBOR: They're still beating hell out of each other.

FATHER: Pity they have tanks now. In the old days I could have made a good thing out of this. Just think of all those nags lying around! . . .

NEIGHBOR: They've reached the top of the beach. You should be able to see them from here.

FATHER: Ah, who gives a hoot? (*Shrugs, but goes to the window.*) Wow, what a crowd! Incredible!

NEIGHBOR: Yes, there must be at least fifty of them.

FATHER: And how are the others taking it?

NEIGHBOR: The Jerries? They're not at all happy. Well, you can imagine! Being dragged out of bed at that hour of the morning! . . .

FATHER: Ah, but you see, local time in America is different from here. Something to do with meridians.

NEIGHBOR: You needn't bother to explain. We all know you used to be a mechanical engineer. How's Marie?

FATHER: Ah, yes . . . That's important. In fact I wanted to ask your advice . . .

ANDRE *returns*.

ANDRE: I couldn't find Marie.

FATHER: I told you not to go to look for her.

ANDRE: Obviously that's why I couldn't find her. Why couldn't you say so at the time? (*He shrugs his shoulders, annoyed.*)

NEIGHBOR: Excuse me, but . . . you said you wanted to ask my advice?

FATHER: Yes, I do. It's like this: Marie is in love with her Heinz.

NEIGHBOR: Her Jerry?

FATHER: Yes, the one who is billeted here.

NEIGHBOR: Ah! And she sleeps with him?

FATHER (*embarrassed*): I don't know. Does she sleep with him, André?

ANDRE (*embarrassed*): I don't know.

FATHER: You see, we don't know. In any case, she does love him, doesn't she, André?

ANDRE: Oh yes, she loves him all right.

FATHER: Then he must love her too.

NEIGHBOR: Get them married. Two people in love ought to get married.

FATHER: Oh, you are bright, aren't you? Do you imagine that hadn't occurred to us?

NEIGHBOR: Well, why didn't you get it over with, then? If they haven't got hitched yet, it's because you didn't think of it! . . .

A shattering explosion. They all duck their heads.

FATHER: That's it.

ANDRE: What's "it"?

FATHER: I don't know. But judging by the din, that was it all right. Anyhow, to get back to my problem. What do you advise me to do?

NEIGHBOR: Marry them off. It hits you in the eye, I'd say. Clear as crystal.

FATHER: Those are metaphors.

NEIGHBOR (*angrily*): And to hell with your quotations, too!

ANDRE: They love each other, all right. That's the size of it.

FATHER: I don't think Heinz would make a good knacker. He's too skinny. But we could train him to sharpen the plane blade.

ANDRE (*delighted*): That's a great idea.

NEIGHBOR: Even so, we ought to know whether or not he's sleeping with her . . .

FATHER: You're right. How can we find out? (*To* ANDRE:) Go and fetch my daughter.

ANDRE: Yes. Right away. (*He goes out.*)

FATHER: It's a damn nuisance, having to think of all these things. How can one get a good night's sleep with such worries to cope with? . . .

Sudden loud burst of machine-gun fire.

NEIGHBOR: What did you say?

FATHER (*shouting above the din*): How can one get a good night's sleep with such worries to cope with?

NEIGHBOR (*shouting*): To start with, you shouldn't be sleeping at this time of day.

FATHER: I know, I know. But this whole marriage business is upsetting me. All I want is a bit of peace and quiet so I can get on with my work.

Knocking at the door.

Come in!

Enter a GERMAN SOLDIER, *carrying a rifle and a bazooka, and drawing a field gun behind him.*

GERMAN SOLDIER: May I stack all this stuff here? It slows me down when I'm running away. And if I leave it just anywhere, somebody's bound to swipe it . . .

FATHER: Yes, yes. Go ahead. No one will touch it.

GERMAN SOLDIER: Thanks. I'll pick it all up on my way back.

FATHER: See you later, then.

The GERMAN SOLDIER *closes the door behind him, and the* FATHER *turns to the* NEIGHBOR *again.*

I hope that idiot André manages to find Marie.

NEIGHBOR: Which Marie?

FATHER: The one who's supposed to marry Heinz.

NEIGHBOR: Ah, yes. It's not very practical, you know, both of them having the same name . . .

FATHER: Too true. And with their mother's name being Marie, as well . . .

NEIGHBOR: How on earth do you know who's who?

FATHER: Well, luckily they all seem to know who they are. Though how, I don't know.

Enter ANDRE.

ANDRE: I can't think where she can be.

FATHER: Did you look for her in her bedroom?

ANDRE: Couldn't. Heinz was in there already.

FATHER: Oh well, that's that, then. Listen, this is a nuisance.

ANDRE: Yes, it is, isn't it.

NEIGHBOR: But you don't have to know all the intimate details immediately.

FATHER: I'd have preferred to. In any case, one thing is quite clear: I shall have to call a family council. And that's going to be quite a problem.

NEIGHBOR: Why? It's a daily routine with most families.

FATHER: Not with my stupid bunch of children fighting in every corner of the earth instead of staying at home and learning the knacker's trade.

NEIGHBOR: Well, they have their job to do, you know. And you shouldn't speak like that about your own children.

FATHER: You don't understand. Jacques, now, he's an American, and his sister Catherine, she's in some Godforsaken spot miles from anywhere.

NEIGHBOR: I thought they were both sons . . .

FATHER: Catherine is a paratrooper in the Red Army, which is more or less the same as being a man.

NEIGHBOR: Ah yes, under those circumstances . . . hmm! I quite agree.

FATHER: In fact, they are both paratroopers.

ANDRE: But listen, how come they're all working for different countries?

FATHER: You and your stupid questions! How do I know? That's how it is. You simply accept with good grace the children that God has given you.

ANDRE: What were you doing at the time? Taking a nap?

FATHER: At the time? What time?

ANDRE: While God was giving you children.

FATHER: Cutting up horses, of course. Or else repairing my plane. What else would I be doing?

ANDRE: How are you going to let them know about the family council?

FATHER: Hmm. We'll have to think about that. Ah, I've got an idea . . . Now why don't you go and ask . . .

Knocking at the door.

Come in!

Enter an AMERICAN SOLDIER.

AMERICAN SOLDIER: Bonjour! Anything pour boire around here?

FATHER: Of course. Everything all right?

AMERICAN SOLDIER: Okay. Thirsty work.

ANDRE *takes a glass, goes to fill it up and presents it to him.*

FATHER (*smugly*): They're giving you a hot time of it, eh?

AMERICAN SOLDIER (*shakes his head*): Uh huh . . . except that those bastards are shooting with real bullets. (*He drinks.*)

FATHER (*impressed*): You don't say! (*Whistles.*) They *have* got a nerve. Real bullets, eh?

AMERICAN SOLDIER: Look. (*He shows his helmet, which has an enormous hole in the back.*)

FATHER (*admiringly*): Well, what do you know!

NEIGHBOR: How come you're still alive?

AMERICAN SOLDIER: Oh, it belongs to a pal. We traded helmets: this one's a darn sight lighter and better ventilated with the hole in it. (*Silence. He yawns and stretches his limbs.*)

Sound of a whistle blowing in the distance.

Well, time to go, I guess. They've just blown half-time.

ANDRE: But you're coming back?

AMERICAN SOLDIER: Sure. (*He produces a small package from his pocket and hands it to* ANDRE.) Here. Be my guest. It'll cure your halitosis.

ANDRE: Thanks. Thanks very much . . . See you again . . .

Exit AMERICAN SOLDIER.

FATHER: What is it?

ANDRE: Chewing gum . . . It says so on the label.

FATHER: Oh, chewing gum. You can dump that in the pit right away. Hey, did you notice?

ANDRE (*throwing the chewing gum into the knacker's pit*): What?

FATHER: He spoke French when he first came in.

NEIGHBOR: Yes, that's right, by golly! He must be a spy.

The FATHER *unhooks his crossbow from the wall, goes to the door, aims carefully and shoots. A sound of breaking glass.*

ANDRE: Was that his helmet or the cucumber frames?

FATHER: His helmet.

NEIGHBOR: Yes, American junk always makes that kind of a noise when it falls to bits.

FATHER (*reflectively*): Then . . . maybe . . . he's not a spy, after all . . .

ANDRE: Hmm! Perhaps not . . .

FATHER: Well, it's a good thing that it was only the cucumber frames that got hit. (*He goes over to hang up his crossbow again.*) I should have asked him if he knew my son Jacques.

NEIGHBOR: What, the one who's an American paratrooper?

FATHER: Yes.

ANDRE: The snag is that there seem to be a lot of them scrambling up the beach.

FATHER: Then we're sure to find at least one who knows Jacques.

Enter his daughter, MARIE.

Ah, there you are, Marie!

NEIGHBOR: Good day, Marie. Well, I gather you want to marry a Jerry. You seem to have fallen in love in a great hurry!

MARIE: To start with, it's not me, it's my sister.

FATHER: Yes, of course. Her sister. And in any case . . . "a great hurry" is a slight exaggeration. After all, they've been sleeping together for four years. (*To* MARIE:) Was Heinz in your room?

MARIE: No, no, dad, he's in my sister's room.

FATHER: That's right. I can't think straight with all this racket going on.

NEIGHBOR: I just don't know how you can tell the two girls apart when they have the same name.

FATHER: As you can see, I can't.

ANDRE: Shall I go and look for her now?

FATHER: No, I'll call her. (*He goes to the inside door, on the left, half opens it and calls out. Reply from off-stage. He returns.*) She's coming.

NEIGHBOR: Good. We'll soon get this all straightened out.

MARIE: Do I have to stay?

FATHER: Naturally. After all, it's to do with your sister's marriage.

MARIE: I think Heinz is a creep.

ANDRE: Me too.

FATHER: Listen, it's not nice to be rude about your sister's fiancé. The young man didn't choose his own face, after all, did he?

MARIE: Well, he made a great mistake in allowing someone else to do the choosing for him. Especially someone with such incredibly bad taste. Ugh! He's all sort of shriveled up, he's skinny, he wears glasses, and his feet smell.

NEIGHBOR: In a house like this, I really don't see how you can tell that his feet smell.

FATHER: You're always beefing to me about that. Look: you can't be a knacker and live in an atmosphere of jasmine and roses . . .

NEIGHBOR: All right, all right. I'm not saying it smells any worse than usual here, it's simply that I can't get used to it.

MARIE: In any case, Heinz has smelly feet.

ANDRE: It's their boots . . . and then, they never change their underwear.

MARIE: He's covered with pimples and he can't dance.

FATHER: But for goodness' sake, it's your sister he's in love with, not you!

MARIE: Good luck to her. I've got nothing against him, it's simply that I couldn't bear the idea of marrying him myself. Just having him as a brother-in-law is bad enough.

Enter the MOTHER.

MOTHER: You called me?

FATHER: No. I was calling Marie.

MOTHER: Well, here I am.

ANDRE: I'll go and look for her. (*He goes out.*)

The NEIGHBOR *mops his brow.*

FATHER: You may as well know that we are in the process of discussing whether or not to call a family council. To decide about this marriage between Heinz and Marie.

MOTHER: They're going to get married? My children! . . . (*She bursts into tears.*)

FATHER (*patting her on the back*): Now, now, don't get all worked up. Have you milked the cows yet?

MOTHER: Why do you ask me that?

FATHER: To take your mind off things.

MOTHER: As a matter of fact, I haven't. I completely forgot. I'll go and milk them right away. (*She starts toward the door, wiping her eyes as she goes, then comes to an abrupt halt.*) By the way, do you know where the iron is? I can never milk the cows properly without the iron . . .

FATHER: It's with the milking-stool, on the shelf.

MOTHER: Oh, good. Well, I'll go and find it then. (*She goes out.*)

NEIGHBOR: Your wife is full of energy.

FATHER: Yours too.

NEIGHBOR: Both our wives are full of energy.

Silence. Explosions, followed by banging on the door. Enter a GERMAN SOLDIER.

GERMAN SOLDIER (*myopic, wearing glasses, rifle slung across his back*): Listen, you people live here, so maybe you can tell me: are all those folk landing over there really Americans?

FATHER: Landing where?

GERMAN SOLDIER (*pointing the direction with his finger*): Over there.

FATHER: Well, of course they're Americans. Who did you think they were? Italians?

GERMAN SOLDIER (*closing the door behind him as he leaves*): Thanks very much.

MARIE: Ooh, I liked *him*!

NEIGHBOR: You hardly saw him. And in any case he was wearing glasses.

MARIE: Mmmm, but those gorgeous muscles!

FATHER: You know what, you're just jealous of your sister. Just because she's happy, practically engaged, probably going to get married, you're jealous. Ah, that's not a nice attitude, you know. Still, I suppose it's understandable on a day like today.

NEIGHBOR: Why on a day like today?

FATHER: Well, it isn't every day a man decides to marry off his daughter, or his daughter's sister, or arrange a mass wedding. You see, I'm even forgetting my own work. (*He goes up to the workbench and picks up his plane.*) I really ought to go down and chop up a few horses. There are four animals ready to go, and they're not even dressed yet.

NEIGHBOR: What, you dress them up now?

FATHER: Oh, what a bore you are. I spend my life explaining technical terms to you. Dressed means planed, trimmed, beaten out, and so on. It's like when you're a mechanic: you beat out your parts on a plate.

NEIGHBOR (*shuddering*): What a horrible idea!

FATHER: Oh, don't be an old fool. An iron plate on a fitter's bench. You're just prejudiced, like everyone else. I suppose you're astonished that I'm still around.

NEIGHBOR: It had occurred to me to wonder why a great

strapping fellow like you wasn't in the thick of the fighting.

FATHER: I know. That's what everybody wonders. The fact is, they forgot all about me.

NEIGHBOR: Didn't they ever send you a greetings card? You know, the thing that starts off "Greetings from the President . . ."?

FATHER: Oh yes, but I never opened the envelope. So I said to myself: they've forgotten me. And that's just what it was: they'd forgotten me.

NEIGHBOR: Didn't anyone come here looking for you?

FATHER: Well, some character did turn up one day, but he had the bad luck to fall into the pit. And after that no one else came.

NEIGHBOR: What did you do with him?

FATHER: With the character? What do you think I did with him? I cut him up, of course. One more or less . . .

NEIGHBOR: It's disgraceful, all the same. Especially when one sees all those Jerries running around half-starved, and there you are, weighing a ton and just bursting with horrible health . . .

FATHER: Oh, I'm not as healthy as all that, you know. (*He coughs.*) Listen, you can hear, I'm coughing.

NEIGHBOR: Me too. (*He coughs.*)

FATHER: So what? Everyone around here coughs.

NEIGHBOR: It's all because of your damned knacker's pit.

Of course people's lungs rot away, breathing in that stink every day of their lives.

FATHER: That's it! That's typical of you! Nag, nag, nag. You can't let five minutes pass without bringing that up. A fine friend you are, I must say. I can't remember a single day when you haven't made fun of me because of the smell.

NEIGHBOR: You're wrong. Last Sunday.

FATHER: That doesn't count. You didn't come around last Sunday.

NEIGHBOR: Maybe not. But I still spent the whole day coughing. (*He coughs.*)

FATHER: What on earth is André doing? He should have found her by now.

During the previous conversation, MARIE *has been coming and going, bringing in and rearranging an extraordinary variety of objects.*

MARIE: It's very difficult to see into Marie's room. He's probably busy enlarging the hole in the floor above.

FATHER: What a life! I change that floor board every day, and the next morning there's always a new hole in it!

MARIE: You'd do better to take the floor board out for good.

Silence. Then banging on the door, accompanied by sounds of machine-gun fire, running and curses.

FATHER: Come in!

Enter a SECOND AMERICAN SOLDIER.

Hello.

AMERICAN SOLDIER: Hi there! Do you have any pen-pals around here?

FATHER: Any what?

AMERICAN SOLDIER: Pen-pals. I'm looking for a pen-pal.

FATHER: What for?

AMERICAN SOLDIER (*blushing*): Euh . . .

MARIE: Now you've made him blush, dad. That's horrid of you.

FATHER: What do you mean, horrid of me? I can't say anything around here without all of you jumping on me.

AMERICAN SOLDIER: So, have you got one?

FATHER: You must be out of your mind! It's easy to see that *you've* only just landed! Listen, the Jerries have been here for four years. Understand? Or are you a complete idiot?

AMERICAN SOLDIER: I'm nineteen years old, and my name is Vladimir Krowski.

MARIE: And what kind of a pen-pal do you want?

AMERICAN SOLDIER: Someone like you.

MARIE: Hey, those are cute! Will you give them to me?

AMERICAN SOLDIER: What?

> MARIE *goes up to him and fingers the insignia stamped "U.S." pinned to his lapels.*

MARIE: Your clips.

AMERICAN SOLDIER: Oh, I can't, I'd be in the brig right away.

MARIE (*rubs herself up against him*): Oh, go on, give them to me . . . Be sweet . . .

FATHER: Look, if we're in your way, we'll go.

MARIE: Yes. Please do. Just five minutes alone, huh?

Exit FATHER *and* NEIGHBOR.

MARIE: So you don't have a pen-pal?

AMERICAN SOLDIER: Sure I do, in America. But that's a long way away.

MARIE: Oh, you're so smartly dressed. Just take them off, huh?

AMERICAN SOLDIER (*retreating*): What? Take what off?

MARIE (*wheedling*): Your clips . . . Go on . . . If you give them to me, I promise I'll become your pen-pal. Wait a minute, though: why do you want a pen-pal?

AMERICAN SOLDIER: Well, to send her parcels, of course. The PX is so overloaded with foodstuffs, we've just got to get rid of some of it.

MARIE: But don't you eat it all yourselves?

AMERICAN SOLDIER: Gee no! It's terrible stuff. Mountains of canned food and chocolate bars. I'm not kidding. There's so much of it that we can hardly advance any more. Sometimes we get our tanks to crush it into the ground, but that takes time.

MARIE: Throw it all away.

AMERICAN SOLDIER: I thought you'd be glad to have some of it.

MARIE: What would I do with things like that? We only eat horsemeat in this house.

AMERICAN SOLDIER: You could sell it to the Germans.

MARIE: They're not that crazy. They'd simply take it without paying for it.

AMERICAN SOLDIER: Hell, you mean we may as well just give them the whole mess?

MARIE: Of course. It's the only solution. And is that all you wanted to do with your pen-pal—give her food parcels?

AMERICAN SOLDIER: Well, yes. What else can we do with all that canned food?

MARIE (*gives him a shove, he climbs onto the table, she follows him*): I'm not talking about the canned food, I'm talking about pen-pals. Do you think I'm attractive?

AMERICAN SOLDIER: Listen, I can't give you my insignia.

MARIE: Never mind. (*A pause.*) What do you do with your American pen-pal when you're back home?

AMERICAN SOLDIER: I take her out. We go to the movies.

MARIE: You kiss her?

AMERICAN SOLDIER (*getting down from the other side of the table*): I can't tell you. Decent people don't discuss that sort of thing. (*A pause.*) What am I going to do about all this canned food?

MARIE: Leave it here, if it worries you so much.

AMERICAN SOLDIER: Gee, thanks! That's swell of you. I'll go and get the cartons.

He starts to leave, but MARIE *holds him back by one arm.*

MARIE: Do you kiss her?

AMERICAN SOLDIER: I'd never have believed a girl could be so forward. Still, mom did warn me about French women.

MARIE: You're a hypocrite. I know perfectly well that you kiss her, and go to bed with her, too.

AMERICAN SOLDIER: I most certainly don't! Anything else, but not that!

MARIE: Oh, go on, go and get your cartons of canned food. And you can keep your silly old clips.

The AMERICAN SOLDIER *goes out, looking offended. She calls through the door:*

Dad! You can come in now . . .

Enter the FATHER *and the* NEIGHBOR.

FATHER: Well, did you get those things you call clips?

MARIE: We're engaged.

NEIGHBOR: Well, that's fine! Now, maybe, we'll have a little peace. Only one more to get married!

FATHER: Who's that?

NEIGHBOR: Catherine, of course!

FATHER: Ah, yes. I keep forgetting that she's not a boy. So you like this American of yours?

MARIE: He's absolutely sweet. He insisted we get engaged right away.

FATHER: That's fine! At least it didn't take *you* four years to find a husband. Where's he gone, then?

MARIE: To get his baggage.

FATHER: Well, well. So Marie's getting married as well. This is going to be an impressive ceremony: two weddings in one day.

Sounds of explosions, people running, then a pounding at the door.

Come in!

The door opens. A head peers through—that of a GERMAN SOLDIER.

GERMAN SOLDIER: Oh, I beg your pardon!

The door closes again. Howls of pain in German.

MARIE: They all seem very excitable today.

Enter ANDRE.

NEIGHBOR: So, André, what's going on?

ANDRE: I don't know what she's doing. Heinz is still in her room.

FATHER: It doesn't matter. I'll have a word with her later. (*He goes over to the radio and starts twirling the dials.*)

MARIE: It's not the right time.

NEIGHBOR: Oh yes, it is. (*He looks at his watch.*)

Sounds of static from the radio.

FATHER: It seems difficult to get the BBC at the moment.

NEIGHBOR: It's this confounded landing, getting nowhere. Static on the beaches and static in the air.

The "Third Man" theme can be heard.

There you are. That's London. It *was* the right time, you see.

FATHER: Good! I can't work without music.

NEIGHBOR (*slapping his forehead*): But of course! I've just thought! We'll telephone the postmistress.

FATHER: Why?

NEIGHBOR: So that she can let your other children know!

The music continues in the background.

FATHER: Yes, that's a good idea. Ask her to step across, will you?

The NEIGHBOR goes off to telephone. Meanwhile the FATHER goes over to his workbench and starts banging away at his plane with a hammer. The MOTHER enters from the door on the left.

By the way, Marie! Did you know? Your daughter's going to marry an American.

MOTHER (*bursting into tears*): My little girl! . . . Come to my arms!

MARIE *throws herself into her mother's arms.*

NEIGHBOR (*returning*): What a miracle! For once she has identified the right daughter!

FATHER: Come, come. Don't cry like that. Have you milked the cows?

MOTHER: Yes, of course. (*She jumps in the air.*) What am I thinking about? I've left the iron turned on. I'll go and unplug it. (*She runs out, then returns.*) You know, they take up much less space once they have been ironed.

FATHER: Who do?

MOTHER: The cows. (*She goes toward the outside door.*) I don't know why I didn't think of it before. (*She goes out.*)

NEIGHBOR: Ah, I can see the postmistress coming.

FATHER: So what message are we going to send the children? We must have something ready by the time she gets here.

NEIGHBOR: That doesn't give us very long, since the post office is just across the street.

FATHER: Exactly. We must think quickly.

All three think quickly.

Think quicker, André.

Enter the POSTMISTRESS *from the left.*

POSTMISTRESS: Well, I couldn't have been prompter, could I?

FATHER: Of course not. You came in from stage left. Anyway, how are things with you?

POSTMISTRESS: I'm getting tired of combing broken plaster out of my hair.

NEIGHBOR: Yes, me too.

POSTMISTRESS: The whole place is falling around my ears.

FATHER: I don't know how *you're* managing, but I find it all very peaceful around here.

Loud noises outside. Two AMERICAN SOLDIERS *come running in and close the door behind them.*

FIRST AMERICAN SOLDIER: I owe you ten bucks.

SECOND AMERICAN SOLDIER: Yeah, fork up.

FIRST AMERICAN SOLDIER: Okay. Here's three pounds sterling. Give me fifty Italian lire change.

They exchange banknotes and coins.

FATHER (*apparently angry*): Good day, gentlemen!

AMERICAN SOLDIERS (*in unison*):

> Happy birthday to you,
> Happy birthday to you,
> Happy birthday, dear Froggies,
> Happy birthday to you.

FATHER: Listen, you're the fifth bunch of people to come banging on my door. We're engaged in important discussions here. What the devil do *you* want?

AMERICAN SOLDIERS (*together*): Gee, I'm sorry! . . . Please excuse us . . . Very impolite, I know . . . But we all wanted . . . me and my buddies . . . to visit a genuine old French farmhouse . . . So here we are . . .

FATHER: Did you have to choose mine?

FIRST AMERICAN SOLDIER: It's the only house still standing.

NEIGHBOR: Christ! You mean you idiots have flattened my house? (*He hurries out.*)

FATHER: All right, all right. Since you're here you may as well stay. But it's a damn nuisance, all the same, if every time troops decide to land at Arromanches they all have to make their way straight to this house, under one stupid pretext or another . . .

POSTMISTRESS: I wouldn't have thought Yanks would have been very interested in a tumbledown old shack like this.

MARIE: My, they're well built, those two. (*She goes up to them.*)

FIRST AMERICAN SOLDIER: Gee, you're swell. Would you care for some K rations?

SECOND AMERICAN SOLDIER: Or some Hershey bars?

MARIE: I'd rather have your clips.

AMERICAN SOLDIERS (*together*): Our what?

MARIE: Your clips. That's English, isn't it?

SECOND AMERICAN SOLDIER (*pondering*): Not as far as I know.

FATHER: Well, do you want to be shown around the building or not?

MARIE: Those things there. (*She points to the insignia on their lapels.*)

SECOND AMERICAN SOLDIER: Heck, no, you can't have our lapel insignia. We'd get into trouble. Come on, mac, let's tour the joint.

FATHER: Off you go, then. Go up the stairs and you'll find yourselves on the first floor. Got it? On top of that there's the attic. Go up, have a look, and come down again. On the ground floor, there's the knacker's yard outside, and underneath it runs the other end of the knacker's pit. It has a trap door, too. By the way, what do you think of them?

FIRST AMERICAN SOLDIER: Of whom?

FATHER: The Fritzes. The Krauts . . . The Germans, I mean. A peculiar crowd, don't you think? . . . Huh? . . . Well, I find them rather strange, anyhow.

FIRST AMERICAN SOLDIER: Germans? Around here?

FATHER: Of course! The place is jam-packed with them.

SECOND AMERICAN SOLDIER: Jesus! Now I understand why they made us land here! . . . To fight the Germans! you'd think they'd have told us! . . .

FIRST AMERICAN SOLDIER: Yeah, you're darned right. So that's why those guys were firing at us. No kidding, these operations are really top secret.

SECOND AMERICAN SOLDIER: Yeah, that's democracy.

They both spring to attention and sing "Happy Birthday to You."

FATHER: Does democracy really work?

FIRST AMERICAN SOLDIER: Impossible to find out. It's top secret.

MARIE: Be sweet. Give me those little shiny brass things.

SECOND AMERICAN SOLDIER: We've already said no. Don't you understand plain English?

MARIE: I'll come with you and show you around upstairs.

POSTMISTRESS: That's right. Go along with them. It will calm you down a bit.

ANDRE: I'll go too.

FATHER: You stay here. We haven't yet decided what message we're going to send.

The AMERICAN SOLDIERS and MARIE go toward the staircase. The FATHER calls them back.

Hey, you there . . . it's just occurred to me . . .

They stop. One of the American soldiers is openly fondling Marie's bottom.

SECOND AMERICAN SOLDIER: What?

FATHER: Do you know my son Jacques?

SECOND AMERICAN SOLDIER: Which branch of the services?

FATHER: He's a paratrooper.

SECOND AMERICAN SOLDIER (*thinking*): Jacques . . . Jacques . . . Jacques, no, I don't remember his name. What color is his parachute?

FATHER: Blue, bright blue.

SECOND AMERICAN SOLDIER: No. Ours are yellow.

FATHER: Ah well, never mind! I just thought I'd ask.

The AMERICAN SOLDIERS *leave the room with* MARIE.

It's up to us three.

ANDRE: I'm thinking. Suppose we sent a message? Something like this? "Return immediately family council re marriage Marie"?

POSTMISTRESS: That's not very original. It's practically a telegram.

FATHER: The BBC would never accept it, anyway. We'll have to send them a message in clear language, not code. (*He thinks.*)

ANDRE: I can't think of anything.

FATHER: Wait . . . I've got it! . . . "The knacker of Arromanches awaits the arrival of his two children to attend their sister's wedding." As I say, it's got to be clear, this message, otherwise people may misunderstand it, and use it as an excuse to ransack the whole town, and do dreadful things like taking the engines out of front-wheel-drive cars and dumping them in the trunk after painting them white.

POSTMISTRESS: Right. I'll try to establish communication with London. But it's going to take at least an hour, you know, before I'll be able to get through. There's a whole line of officers waiting their turn at my counter right now, and I already have three cables for Berlin and five for London. So it's bound to take time . . .

Violent banging on the door. Enter two GERMAN SOLDIERS *in uniform.*

POSTMISTRESS: How do you do?

GERMAN SOLDIERS (*together*): How do you do? How's business?

FATHER: Not too good. It could be better. We're all tied up at present with this problem of Marie's marriage . . .

ANDRE: Business is just so-so.

FIRST GERMAN SOLDIER: May we sit down? We're pooped out.

FATHER: Of course. Take a chair.

The Germans sit down at a table near the door. The SECOND GERMAN SOLDIER *starts taking off his boots. The* FIRST GERMAN SOLDIER *goes out, fills his helmet with water, then returns and soaks his feet in it, keeping his boots on. The* SECOND GERMAN SOLDIER *puts his boots on the table. Thick steam starts rising from them. Nobody pays any attention to any of this activity.*

Well, are you going to send this message?

POSTMISTRESS: How about pouring me a slug of red-eye before I go?

FATHER: Of course. I'm all mixed up today. And I'm not

even getting any work done. (*He goes toward the cupboard.*)

POSTMISTRESS: Don't worry, I'll send your message off soon. I'll drink up quickly.

Footsteps can be heard descending the staircase. The two AMERICAN SOLDIERS *appear, completely disheveled, through the door on the right. The two* GERMAN SOLDIERS *get up, count to four, and sing a marching song.*)

GERMAN SOLDIERS (*in unison*):

Wenn die Soldaten
Durch die Stadt marschieren
Offnen die Mädchen
Die Fenster und die Türen.
Ein Warum, Ein Darum, Ein Warum, Ein Darum,
Ein Küss wenn es stimmt darassabum darassassa.

(*Repeat.*)

FATHER: Well, how do you like the house?

FIRST AMERICAN SOLDIER (*buttoning up his pants*): It stinks to hell here, it stinks worse than any house I've ever been in. Ugh!

SECOND AMERICAN SOLDIER: That's the cause of it. (*He points to the two boots placed on the table by the* SECOND GERMAN, *which are still steaming.*)

FATHER: Something to drink?

FIRST AMERICAN SOLDIER: Say, those boots are just darling.

SECOND AMERICAN SOLDIER: They sure carry weird gear,

those krauts. Look at their guns—quite different from
our Colts.

FIRST GERMAN SOLDIER (*in a condescending tone*): Your
pistols aren't too bad.

The two AMERICAN SOLDIERS *walk up to the table
where the Germans are sitting and lean on the backs
of their chairs.*

SECOND AMERICAN SOLDIER: Get a load of those helmets!

SECOND GERMAN SOLDIER: I quite agree that the shape is
really terrible . . . Unesthetic. Unattractive.

SECOND AMERICAN SOLDIER: How about a hand of poker?

FATHER (*coming up*): Listen, you four must be thirsty.
How about a shot of calvados?

FIRST GERMAN SOLDIER: Certainly. Thank you.

SECOND GERMAN SOLDIER: With pleasure.

FIRST AMERICAN SOLDIER: Sure.

SECOND AMERICAN SOLDIER: Dandy idea.

FATHER: André, bring some glasses.

FIRST GERMAN SOLDIER: Do you have a pack of cards on
you?

FIRST AMERICAN SOLDIER: Yeah, I always carry a deck.

POSTMISTRESS (*coming up unobtrusively, and swallowing
her drink at the same time*): Fill my glass. We'll
drink a toast with these boys.

The four soldiers start playing cards.

FIRST AMERICAN SOLDIER: I'll play you for your boots.

SECOND GERMAN SOLDIER: Right. Against your jacket.

FIRST AMERICAN SOLDIER: Okay.

Card game, during which they all gradually undress, finishing up by wearing each other's uniforms.

FATHER: No doubt about it. A little drink perks one up. (*He goes over to his workbench and starts hammering at his plane, banging away at it with a noise that gradually rises to a crescendo.*)

FIRST GERMAN SOLDIER: Full house—aces high.

POSTMISTRESS: Well, I'll be off. Good-by, gentlemen.

The four soldiers rise in unison, holding onto their pants.

FOUR SOLDIER: (*together*): Good-by, madam. - - -Bye, ma'am.

SECOND AMERICAN SOLDIER: I'll see you!

FIRST GERMAN SOLDIER: That makes the pot.

SECOND GERMAN SOLDIER: I'll open for ten dollars.

SECOND AMERICAN SOLDIER: And twenty marks.

FATHER (*accompanying the* POSTMISTRESS *to the side door*): And try to get through to London right away, will you? Thanks.

Explosions can be heard. The noise becomes louder and louder. Violent knocking at the back door. Everyone looks in that direction. The POSTMISTRESS *stands where she is.*

Come in!

FIRST GERMAN SOLDIER: Flush!

SECOND GERMAN SOLDIER: Royal flush!

SECOND AMERICAN SOLDIER: Four aces!

FIRST AMERICAN SOLDIER: Ha! Five kings! (*He scoops up the stakes.*)

> HEINZ *enters by the door on the left. The* FATHER *and the others start in surprise.*

FATHER (*severely*): Now then, Heinz, why aren't you out there fighting alongside your mates?

HEINZ (*blushing*): My alarm clock didn't go off.

> *Terrible explosion. Everybody ducks. Deathly silence. Steps can be heard coming down the stairs.* MARIE *enters.*

MARIE: Dad! Have we any glue? I've just knocked a vase over.

FATHER (*relieved*): Oh, so that's what the noise was. (*Turning back to* HEINZ *and folding his arms.*) A likely story . . .

FIRST AMERICAN SOLDIER: Three queens—twice! (*He scoops up the stakes.*)

FIRST GERMAN SOLDIER: I beat you! Seven-card straight! (*He takes the stake money from the* FIRST AMERICAN SOLDIER.)

SECOND AMERICAN SOLDIER: Whoa there! I'm holding a royal flush, ace right down to deuce! (*He takes the stake money from the* FIRST GERMAN SOLDIER.)

SECOND GERMAN SOLDIER: Well, I've got a genuine pair of kings. (*He starts methodically stripping the clothes off the other three.*)

Meanwhile, HEINZ *is standing there twiddling his thumbs.*

HEINZ (*timidly*): Could you perhaps write a little note of excuse for me to give my captain?

MARIE *approaches the card players. From each side of her, a hand creeps up her skirt.*

FATHER: What a life! Oh, all right. (*He writes a note.*)

Then from outside, bursts of machine-gun fire, detonations, bright flashes. The door blows open.

SECOND GERMAN SOLDIER: Two hundred dollars.

FIRST AMERICAN SOLDIER: And ten marks.

SECOND AMERICAN SOLDIER: I've had enough of this. I'm quitting.

He gets up. He is dressed entirely in German uniform, as is his buddy. They turn on their heels and start marching out of the room, singing "Wenn die Soldaten . . . ," while the two GERMAN SOLDIERS, *dressed entirely in American uniform, turn toward the* FATHER, *sing "Happy Birthday . . ." to him and also start marching out.*

FIRST AMERICAN SOLDIER: Sehr gut!

FIRST GERMAN SOLDIER: Okay!

SECOND AMERICAN SOLDIER: Vorwärts!

SECOND GERMAN SOLDIER: Let's go!

Exit the FOUR SOLDIERS.

FATHER: That was nice of those kids, singing to me.

POSTMISTRESS: Yes . . . How about another shot of that rotgut of yours?

FATHER: You'd better take it easy.

Explosions. Banging on the door.

Come in!

The door opens slowly. A NONDESCRIPT SOLDIER *staggers in, clutching his stomach. Long silence.*

NONDESCRIPT SOLDIER (*gasping for breath*): 'Scuse, please, but where's the can?

FATHER: It's just been canned.

NONDESCRIPT SOLDIER: Ah! . . . Aaaaaaaaaargh! . . . (*He drops dead.*)

FATHER: Into the pit, with full military honors.

The POSTMISTRESS *rolls the corpse of the* NONDESCRIPT SOLDIER *over into the pit.*

Enter the MOTHER.

MOTHER: Hey, the toilet's disappeared.

FATHER: I am aware of that.

MOTHER: Oh well, I'll be off then. You don't need me, do you?

FATHER: I always need you, darling. Come to my arms. (*To the* POSTMISTRESS:) Look, take the bottle of grog and the children, too, and bugger off. I am about to misbehave myself.

POSTMISTRESS: Come on, kiddywinks, let's go and wet our whistles. Today's a holiday!

The POSTMISTRESS *leaves with* MARIE *and* ANDRE, *holding them by the hand like two little children.*

FATHER (*tickling the* MOTHER): Gilly . . . gilly . . . gilly . . .

MOTHER: Hooh! hooh! hooh! Stop it, Joachim . . . Not here, somebody might see us.

FATHER (*annoyed*): My name is not Joachim. You're mixing me up with your first husband. You know—the gamekeeper.

MOTHER: I'm so sorry. It had completely slipped my mind.

FATHER: Well, anyhow, we're going to see our children again. Doesn't that please you?

MOTHER: I'm all mixed up. I don't know what's the matter with me today, but this marriage business worries me, I must say.

FATHER: Ah ha! It reminds you of your own marriage, huh, sweetheart?

MOTHER: Certainly not. I've forgotten my own marriage long ago!

FATHER: Well, really!

MOTHER (*glaring at him*): Do you ever do anything to remind me of the fact that we are married?

FATHER (*embarrassed*): Hmm! It's not as easy as all that, you know. After all, I'm forty-two years old . . .

MOTHER: Well, I'm not!

Heavy silence.

FATHER: Listen, don't you think we should give Marie a different name?

MOTHER: Which Marie?

FATHER: Either of them. Just so long as one of the two gets a different name.

MOTHER: I'm against it.

FATHER: But it would be much more practical.

MOTHER: So you don't like my name.

FATHER: On the contrary . . . I'd like it to be all your own. And, in any case, I think it might be better to give her a new name; Heinz tends to get mixed up between the two and that annoys Marie, because she can't stand the sight of him.

MOTHER: If Marie doesn't love Heinz she's not obliged to marry him.

FATHER: But that's just the point. I was talking about the other Marie. Now you can see how inconvenient the whole arrangement is.

MOTHER: Only because you're a stupid oaf.

The FATHER *lifts his arms, then slaps his thighs in despair.*

Well, it's true! She's been called Marie for fifteen years now, and you suddenly want to change her name. I just can't make you out! You're always coming up with crazy ideas. Why can't you just get on with your job of cutting up horses, and shut up?

FATHER: I'm sick and tired of being a knacker. To start with, I've lost the knack, and secondly, my plane is worn to a frazzle.

MOTHER: You're getting old. Well, do what you want, then. Call her what you like.

FATHER (*delighted*): Come to my arms, my love!

MOTHER (*bursting into tears*): My little girl! . . .

Enter Heinz's MARIE.

FATHER: Ah, here she is! (*To the* MOTHER:) Look, don't cry like that, Marie. It's nothing—just a change of name.

MOTHER: Nothing, huh! She's already going to have to change her surname when she marries her bespectacled idiot, and now you want to change her first name as well. What will she have left?

MARIE: Why are you two arguing?

FATHER: From now on, your first name will be Cyprienne.

MOTHER (*recovering her spirits, astonished and delighted*): Cyprienne? Oh, how lovely!

FATHER (*feigning modesty*): Hmm . . . Well . . . I didn't actually invent the name . . .

MARIE-CYPRIENNE: Cyprienne? That's fine as far as I'm concerned. I don't mind being called Cyprienne, but what on earth is the point?

FATHER: Well, Marie is getting just a bit monotonous.

CYPRIENNE: Yes, I suppose it is rather overused. But Cyprienne Schnittermach . . . does that really sound all right?

FATHER: Certainly.

MOTHER: You may feel a little strange at first, but you'll soon get used to it: it's a beautiful name.

FATHER (*rather flattered*): I must admit it is original.

Silence.

CYPRIENNE: Aren't you working today, dad?

FATHER: Ah no! Today's a special day.

CYPRIENNE: Why, what's happening?

FATHER: Your brother and sister are arriving for a family council.

CYPRIENNE: What family council?

FATHER: About your marriage, of course.

CYPRIENNE: Oh, I see . . . I thought it was about something new.

FATHER: What! You don't find the subject of your marriage new?

CYPRIENNE: I've been sleeping with Heinz for four years.

FATHER: Has he given you a child?

CYPRIENNE: I doubt it. I'd have noticed.

FATHER: Are you or are you not pregnant?

CYPRIENNE (*walking up and down, humming*): What's that got to do with you?

MOTHER: You owe us an answer, you know, Cyprienne . . . (*Dreamily.*) Cyprienne . . . I'd have liked to have been called that.

CYPRIENNE: You both make me sick with your stupid questions. You've peeked through the hole in the floor quite often enough to have found out whether or not the things I do with Heinz are likely to have left me pregnant.

FATHER: How on earth are we to tell? First, you always turn out the light when things start to get interesting. Second, you oil the bedsprings. And lastly, it's André who spies on you, not me. I put in a new floor board every day, as you know quite well.

CYPRIENNE: Come off it! You always put on your floor-board replacement act at ten o'clock at night . . . just after we've gone to bed.

FATHER: What a disgusting suggestion. God knows such thoughts never enter my mind.

MOTHER: God knows better, and so do I.

FATHER: In any case, you should tell us whether or not you are pregnant.

CYPRIENNE: Oh, go to hell!

Crashing noise from the attic. A trap door opens, and a paratrooper floats down to the ground. It is the knacker's son JACQUES.

MOTHER: Why, it's my little Jacques!

JACQUES: Hi, everybody!

Hugs and kisses all around.

MOTHER: My little Jacques! Oh, it's been such a long time since you last came home to visit your old dad and your mom! (*She bursts into tears.*)

FATHER: Hey, there! Why "your *old* dad"?

JACQUES: You haven't changed, huh, mom? Always good for a joke, eh? (*He hugs his* MOTHER.) And how are things with you, Marie, honey?

CYPRIENNE: Hello, Jacques. That's a beautiful tunic you have on.

He kisses her.

JACQUES: Marie's gotten to be quite a dish. (*Whistles.*)

FATHER: You can call her Cyprienne now: she's going to get married.

JACQUES: No kidding! . . . That's great! (*He looks at her with an expression of amazement. Then he sniffs and turns to his father.*) Hmm, still the same old stink around here. Hard at work, eh, dad?

FATHER: The pit is chock-full.

JACQUES (*rubbing his hands together*): Grand! . . .

The overhead trap door opens again and a second paratrooper alights. This time it is a JAPANESE PARA-TROOPER.

JAPANESE PARATROOPER: Hai dōzo dōmo-arigāto-gozāimas ohāyo anonē mushi-mushi.

FATHER (*counting on his fingers*): It's not Jacques. It's not Marie. It's not Catherine. No, it can't be one of my children.

JACQUES: You must have lost your way.

JAPANESE PARATROOPER: Hai dōzo dōmo-arigāto-gozāimas *litely*): Sūmimasēn. Gōmen nasāi. Hiroshima dēska?

FATHER (*politely, smiling*): So sorry, but I don't understand.

JAPANESE PARATROOPER (*draws a dagger from his belt and commits hara-kiri, shouting*): Banzai! . . .

JACQUES: Heck, he really was a Jap! What do we do with him?

FATHER: Into the pit, along with the others.

They pick up the body and throw it into the pit.

MOTHER: Cyprienne, scrub the floor, please—what a mess!

Sound of steps coming down the staircase. Knocking at the right-hand door. Enter CATHERINE *dressed as a Pin-Up Paratrooper of the Red Army: red boots, pleated miniskirt, khaki blouse, red panties. Horribly overdeveloped bust. Red Army cap. A red star over each breast.*

FATHER: Ah, there she is at last!

MOTHER: Welcome home, pet!

Hugs and kisses all around. CATHERINE *kisses her* FATHER *and her brother* JACQUES *on the mouth, Soviet Russian style, which leaves them panting.*

CATHERINE: Well, it's nice to be back again. (*She sniffs the air.*)

MOTHER: I hope you didn't have too much trouble getting here, love?

CATHERINE: Well, it wasn't so easy. It's difficult to recognize locations from that height . . . There seems to have been quite a bit of activity in the old place since I was here last.

FATHER: You're not kidding! Last year, old Durosier had his three elm trees chopped down . . .

MOTHER (*going one better*): And Madame Lecoin has just had a new cathouse built for her pussies—twenty feet long . . .

JACQUES: Ah, yes, that must have altered the landscape. But we still located the old spot, as you see . . . (*He sniffs meaningfully.*)

CATHERINE: So it's you that's engaged, is it, Marie?

CYPRIENNE: You can call me Cyprienne.

CATHERINE: Oh, so they've finally got around to changing your name. About time! Do you like my costume?

CYPRIENNE: Absolutely smashing! Where did you have it made?

CATHERINE: There's a marvelous little dressmaker just behind the Kremlin: she's really a genius, my dear, she runs up costumes for me for almost nothing . . .

They go on gossiping.

JACQUES: And where is Marie?

MOTHER: But she's *there*, sweetheart. I keep on telling you that she is called Cyprienne now.

FATHER: No, no, he means the other Marie, of course. Well, as a matter of fact, she has just got engaged this morning to one of your compatriots, an American. Now that I come to think of it, he hasn't come back, has he? I wonder what he's up to? And where's Marie, for that matter? I suppose she's still at the post office.

Enter MARIE.

MARIE: May I come in?

FATHER: Ah, there she is!

JACQUES (*throwing himself on her and hugging her enthusiastically*): Welcome home, you living doll.

FATHER: Look here, Jacques, leave your sister alone! She's not twelve years old any longer, you know. The way you're behaving, anyone would think you wanted to go to bed with her.

JACQUES: So what? Didn't you ever?

FATHER: Certainly not! You filthy swine!

JACQUES: Oh well, every family has one moron in it, I suppose. (*He laughs.*)

CATHERINE: So where is *your* fiancé, Cyprienne?

CYPRIENNE: Fighting, like most soldiers at this time of day. He was late for work, and dad had to write him a note to take to his captain. They are terribly strict with him.

FATHER: Hey, you scamps, come over here and have a drink. Sit around this table and try to behave yourselves.

They all go over and sit down, arranging themselves

so that CYPRIENNE *is isolated at one end of the table, like a defendant in a trial.* CATHERINE *swallows her drink, then hurls the empty glass against the wall: nobody pays any attention.*

(*Rising.*) Now let's get down to business . . . Cyprienne! . . .

CYPRIENNE: Yes, dad?

FATHER: You are engaged to Heinz. You intend to marry him. You are well aware of the fact that there is no question . . . (*emphasizing each word*) . . . of your getting married without the agreement of the whole family. Consequently, and logically, you are required to answer every question we put to you, giving the precise details which will permit us to formulate an objective judgment on the basis of which we will decide, in the ultimate event, whether or not we deem it appropriate for you to go through with the marriage ceremony. (*He collapses, exhausted.*)

JACQUES (*rising*): You may as well get it into your head right away that we didn't come all this distance for nothing. Consequently, I insist that you give us the exact details of what's been going on, so that we can come to a decision. (*He sits down again.*)

CYPRIENNE (*rising*): I don't know what to say, really; it seems that everybody else has already said everything. (*She sits down again.*)

Everybody looks at CYPRIENNE. *The* FATHER *sits up slowly.*

FATHER: Now, for the last time, answer my question. Ar

you or are you not pregnant as a result of the activities of the aforementioned Heinz Schnittermach?

JACQUES (*rising*): What a ghastly name! (*He sits down again.*)

The MOTHER *bursts into tears.* MARIE *calms her.*

FATHER (*to the* MOTHER): Marie! Did you remember to bring in the big ladder?

MOTHER: My God! . . . I completely forgot . . . (*She scurries off in a panic.*)

FATHER: Cyprienne! Answer me! . . .

CYPRIENNE: You're getting on my nerves. I refuse to answer.

FATHER: In that case we shall have to have recourse to draconian measures, so called from the name of the inventor.

JACQUES: Like "sadistic practices."

FATHER: Marie, go up to your room.

MARIE *starts to go toward the door, followed by* JACQUES.

Jacques! . . . stay here! . . .

CYPRIENNE: Now I see why you made me change my name. Otherwise I'd have gone up to my room as well, and you couldn't have done anything about it.

MARIE *goes out.*

FATHER: Now then, you two, lay her down on the work-bench.

CATHERINE *and* JACQUES *grip* CYPRIENNE.

Take her dress off: we don't want it to get creased.

The dress is removed. Under her peasant costume, CYPRIENNE *is wearing black stockings, and bright red brassiere, garter belt, and panties. They stretch her out on the workbench.*

JACQUES: What shall we use to give her a working over with? (*He laughs fiendishly.*)

CATHERINE: I've got some cigars.

FATHER: I can't stand the smell of cigar smoke.

CATHERINE *shrugs, and starts tying* CYPRIENNE *down on the workbench.*

CYPRIENNE: Nor can I. But I wouldn't want my personal opinion to sway you in the least.

FATHER: When I say that I can't stand the smell of cigar smoke, I'm not simply using a figure of speech. There are two things in this world that I absolutely cannot stand: one is a blunt-edged plane, and the other is having wet feet.

JACQUES: Hey, what about the smell of cigar smoke?

FATHER: Well, that blows away sooner or later, and in any case it would be impossible to smell it in this establishment. I think it would be better if we tried tickling her.

CYPRIENNE *is by now tied down by her wrists and*

ankles and is lying motionless. The FATHER *rummages around for something with which to tickle her.*

JACQUES: Listen, Cyprienne. We didn't come home simply to annoy you, you know. We are asking you a perfectly simple question. If you had answered right away, you would have avoided a scene which is spectacular, I must admit, but also deplorable.

CYPRIENNE: What do you want me to say? . . . You're all hovering around waiting to pounce on me like fleas infesting a mangy dog. Or maybe you are feeling just as embarrassed as I am. Mind you, if I were in your shoes I'd do exactly the same thing, because it's the only way to get me to talk. I'm as obstinate as a mule and I don't feel like answering your question.

JACQUES: Okay then, baby, we're going to have to tickle you.

He goes up to CYPRIENNE *and starts tickling her. She twists and writhes.*

FATHER: Go on, really give it to her. She's as strong as a horse . . . and I know horses. Here, try this rooster's tail feather. There's nothing like it.

JACQUES: Bring me a straw.

CYPRIENNE *screams with pleasure.*

Oh, Cyprienne! . . . For pete's sake, pipe down . . . You're giving me a headache! . . .

CYPRIENNE *screams even louder.*

FATHER: Be careful of that feather, Jacques, I'm very fond

of it. What a pigheaded girl . . . Are you going to answer, you little goose?

CYPRIENNE *goes on howling.*

CATHERINE (*putting on lipstick*): You know, Cyprienne, you disappoint me. I wouldn't have thought you'd be so uncommunicative. I would have expected you to be more trusting and affectionate toward your brother and your sister.

JACQUES (*mopping his brow*): This is just ridiculous. Why do you refuse to answer? See here, you've been shacking up with this character for four years, everyone knows it, and everyone has seen you on the job. And I hasten to add that there is absolutely nothing wrong with that. Yet for some unknown reason, sheer stupidity or spite, I suppose, you refuse to tell us whether or not you are pregnant. It just doesn't make sense. It makes me wonder how you'd react if something really serious happened to you.

CATHERINE: We come home. We are all happy to see you and your fiancé. We are all looking forward to a nice little family reunion with mama and papa (*she wipes away a tear*) and then you refuse to talk to us. You act more like a stranger than a member of the family.

JACQUES (*deeply moved, in a broken voice*): We had every right to expect a better reception than this. (*He sniffs.*)

FATHER (*sobbing*): Cyprienne! . . . My little girl . . . I'd never have thought you would have treated us this way!

CATHERINE (*wipes her eyes furtively and goes to sit down*): Cyprienne, we are all suffering because of you, and yet you just lie there saying nothing.

CYPRIENNE *writhes with laughter.*

FATHER: Hold on, I'll get some nails. Then we can fix her more securely. I don't know why it's the thing to tie people down with cords when it's so much simpler to nail them down.

JACQUES: But that will spoil the workbench.

FATHER: Never mind about that. After all, the workbench doesn't come first in a case like this, when your sister's marriage is at stake. Here's the hammer.

JACQUES: No, I think maybe we'll use adhesive tape.

FATHER: Catherine, go and get it. It's in the tool cupboard.

She goes over to the cupboard, and during the following scene gets horribly entangled in the adhesive tape.

JACQUES: I can't make it, pop . . . I never could stand being tickled . . . and this makes me feel just as though someone were doing it to me . . . Please take over from me, pop . . .

FATHER: Come, come, you should be ashamed of yourself! *You* a hero! In my time, around 1890, it would have been unthinkable for a paratrooper to turn chicken like that.

JACQUES: Yes, and they brought you up like savages.

CYPRIENNE *has yelled herself hoarse, and starts coughing.*

FATHER (*severely*): Jacques, don't make your sister cough. It's not you who has to pay two hundred francs a month for her singing lessons, huh?

JACQUES: Nor you, either?

FATHER: Maybe not, but I had it in mind . . . Now, for goodness' sake, Catherine, stop making a fool of yourself! Oh! These children! . . .

CATHERINE (*hopelessly entangled in the tape*): Help me, dad, cut it for me.

FATHER (*does so, grumbling. To* CYPRIENNE): Answer yes or no: has Heinz made you pregnant?

CATHERINE: Let me take over, dad.

CYPRIENNE: I won't speak, I won't speak . . . Ooh! aah! Leave me alone . . . (*She explodes with laughter.*) Stop, stop! . . . I'll talk . . .

FATHER (*proudly*): She knows all the places, that Catherine! She's a real tomboy. Come now, Cyprienne, are you going to have a baby?

CYPRIENNE: No . . .

JACQUES: Is that true?

CYPRIENNE: Yes . . .

CATHERINE: You're not lying to us?

CYPRIENNE: I'm telling the truth.

FATHER (*collapsing into a chair*): Well, I must say . . . it takes a lot to make you talk.

JACQUES (*in a broken voice*): Give me a drink, pop . . .

They all crowd around him.

CYPRIENNE, *furious, suddenly slaps them one by one without warning. They all stand there, rubbing their cheeks.*

CYPRIENNE: Why did you do that to me? Why did you do that to me? I didn't want to tell . . . Beasts . . .

Knocking at the door.

FATHER: To know if you were obliged to marry Heinz. Now that we know he hasn't impregnated you, we'll have to start from scratch again and remedy the situation as quickly as possible. You are going to marry him this very day. That makes you happy, huh, you idiot! . . .

Knocking redoubled.

Come in!

Enter an ancient Maquis Resistance fighter, wearing a long black beard, and a juvenile Maquis Resistance colonel, age fourteen.

ANCIENT RESISTANCE FIGHTER: Allow me to introduce ourselves. Vincent, known as Whitebeard, French Resistance Forces, and Colonel Loriot.

COLONEL LORIOT: Stand at ease.

FATHER: What can we do for you?

VINCENT: It seems you have a Yank hanging around your house?

COLONEL LORIOT: Yes, we were told that. In any case, we saw him.

FATHER: Ah, that must be my son Jacques. Come in, come in! Make yourselves at home.

VINCENT (*to* JACQUES): So I take it that you've just landed with the American forces?

JACQUES (*modestly*): Oh, I just dropped in to attend my sister's wedding, that's all.

COLONEL LORIOT: What's it like in America?

JACQUES: Hmm . . . I don't really know. I come from around these parts.

VINCENT (*disappointed*): Oh, excuse us. We thought that was an American uniform you're wearing . . .

COLONEL LORIOT: I'm afraid we haven't had much practice. We only joined the Resistance this morning.

FATHER: Have you nabbed my car?

VINCENT: What make is it?

FATHER: A Rollswagen.

COLONEL LORIOT: Front-wheel drive?

VINCENT: No, no, Colonel, don't be a driveling idiot, there's no such thing as a front-wheel-drive Rollswagen . . .

COLONEL LORIOT: Ah . . . Oh well . . .

VINCENT (*explaining*): You see, we are only interested in front-wheel drives.

FATHER: You should take our neighbor's car, then. It's brand new.

COLONEL LORIOT: What's its registration number?

FATHER: 5 4 8 7 6 0 6 0 0 2.

VINCENT: That's it. That's the Colonel's car. But we were looking for one for myself.

FATHER: Sorry I can't help you.

COLONEL LORIOT: Well, never mind.

VINCENT: It's all very well for you, you've already got a car! (*To* JACQUES:) How do those things you call Jeeps work?

JACQUES: I have no idea. I only use a parachute.

VINCENT (*to* CATHERINE): Do you know, miss?

CATHERINE: I'm a paratrooper, too.

VINCENT *and* COLONEL LORIOT (*rising*): Ah . . . well, in that case . . . we'll be off. Good evening, ladies and gentlemen.

FATHER: Good evening, see you again.

VINCENT: A Rollswagen . . . hmm . . . Oh no, we couldn't possibly take that . . . Much too conspicuous.

FATHER: I'm so sorry . . . (*He sees them out.*)

CATHERINE *has finished untying* CYPRIENNE *and takes her toward the staircase.*

(*To* CATHERINE:) Bring Marie back with you.

JACQUES (*still all choked up*): Bring mama back.

CATHERINE: Oh really, Jacques, this is too much. Pull yourself together! If you behave like this at your sister's wedding what on earth will you be like when you get married yourself? (*She goes out.*)

JACQUES: Mama! . . . Mama! . . .

Sounds of activity from the direction of the pit. The NEIGHBOR *emerges, all covered with earth and pschitt and feeling his way out with groping hands.*

FATHER: Hello! Who's that clambering out of my pit? (*He studies him closely.*) Why, it's our neighbor!

NEIGHBOR: My house wasn't flattened at all. I went to see, and there it was, still standing. You can imagine what a shock it gave me. I inspected the whole premises from cellar to attic, just to be sure everything was still in the right place. Or rather, from attic to cellar. Everything was all right.

FATHER: But how come you've just crawled out of my knacker's pit?

NEIGHBOR: Well, that's the whole point. Just as I was going to climb back up from the cellar I heard a loud noise and the cellar ceiling caved in on my nut. So I started digging my way toward you . . . following my nose. (*He sniffs ostentatiously.*) All the same, I'm glad my house hasn't come to any harm. That would have grieved me deeply.

FATHER: Yes, I can understand that.

NEIGHBOR: You'll lend me a hand repairing my cellar ceiling, won't you?

FATHER: Yes, yes, but it will have to wait till tomorrow. As you can see, we're all tied up with our Cyprienne today.

JACQUES (*groaning*): Pop, go and look for mom . . .

FATHER: Yes, yes, lad, I'll call her right away. I was just going to do so.

NEIGHBOR: You shouldn't give in to all his whims.

FATHER: Jacques has always been more sensitive than the others. And in any case, this isn't a whim at all. You don't think we are going to let Cyprienne get married without her mother being present, do you? (*During this speech, he arranges tools on the workbench, then goes up to the door on the right and shouts.*) Marie! . . .

The MOTHER *enters from the door at the back.*

MOTHER: Were you calling? Here I am. (*Suddenly panic-stricken.*) What's the matter? Why is Jacques lying down? (*She bursts into tears.*) An accident. My little boy! . . .

FATHER (*severely*): Tell me, Marie, have you checked whether the third piglet has had its soup?

MOTHER: The third piglet? There's a third piglet and you didn't tell me? I must go and have a look at the little darling.

She trots off toward the exit. The FATHER *catches hold of her.*

FATHER: No, no, stay here, for goodness' sake. I was only joking!

MOTHER (*annoyed*): You're always playing jokes on me . . .

Everybody waits for her to burst into tears, but instead she pulls herself together and delivers a powerful punch to the father's belly.

FATHER (*gasping*): Ouf! . . .

He clutches his stomach and jumps up and down. The MOTHER *stares at her clenched fist with astonishment before letting her arm drop to her side.*

Well, really, Marie! Have you gone clean out of your mind?

MOTHER (*bursting into tears*): It's your fault for teasing me all the time.

JACQUES: Mom! Come and cuddle me.

MOTHER (*rushing up to him*): Yes, yes, darling! Are you all right?

JACQUES: I just wanted to see you, that's all.

She fondles him. The FATHER *staggers toward his workbench. The* NEIGHBOR *is writhing with silent laughter.*

FATHER (*noticing him*): So you think that's funny, do you, you old fossil?

NEIGHBOR (*offended*): Old fossil! . . . I'm exactly the same age as you! . . .

FATHER: You were born three hours before me.

NEIGHBOR (*gloomily*): True! True! (*Silence.*) Could you lend me a tool to scrape some of this dirt off me?

FATHER: You're a pest. You're going to make everything rusty. (*He proffers him a huge nail, grumbling.*)

NEIGHBOR: To hell with miserly, stingy people.

Enter the chorus of the two GERMAN SOLDIERS *and*

the two AMERICAN SOLDIERS. *Their uniforms are by now completely mixed up.*

FIRST AMERICAN SOLDIER: Pardon me, would you care to listen to the song we've just been rehearsing? Ein, zwei . . .

Chorus of "Wenn die Soldaten . . ."

FIRST GERMAN SOLDIER: We thank you for your gracious attention.

The four make deep bows and exit.

MOTHER: Come now, little Jacquot, I've coddled you long enough now . . .

JACQUES: Oh no . . . please go on!

MOTHER: Really, Jacquot, you're too old for all this.

NEIGHBOR: There, I'm more or less clean now.

MOTHER: Why don't the young people have a little dance?

NEIGHBOR (*rising*): What a good idea. I'll go and get my fiddle. (*He leaves the room.*)

FATHER: Look here, Jacques, you've been mollycoddled quite long enough. Get up and help your dad to clear up the room.

MOTHER: Put the table on the left there. I'll set it for the meal right away.

They clear the table. Enter the NEIGHBOR.

NEIGHBOR (*holding a brand-new violin in his hand*): That was a bit of luck, I found it right away. (*To the* FATHER:) Just imagine, it was under the kitchen sink, right in the middle of the sitting room. Listen, when we repair the cellar ceiling we'd better start by dismantling the rest of the house. That way we'll be able to see what we are doing.

FATHER: Yes, yes. We'll talk about that tomorrow. Hey, wait a minute . . . (*He is struck by a sudden idea.*)

NEIGHBOR: What?

FATHER: You'll be able to claim War Damage . . .

They both laugh until they are out of breath.

Enter CATHERINE, *with* MARIE *who has now changed into a very tarty dress.*

MARIE: Oh, you've been rearranging the room. (*Clapping her hands.*) Are we going to have a dance?

MOTHER: Is that your new dress you have on?

MARIE: The other got torn . . .

NEIGHBOR: Right, take your places for the square dance. (*He takes his violin and starts playing a lively tune.*)

FATHER: Hey, Catherine, come and dance with me.

NEIGHBOR: The betrothed couple should really open the ball.

MOTHER: I'll go and see if I can find them.

FATHER: I'll phone Heinz myself. (*To the* MOTHER:) Where abouts is he fighting at the moment?

MOTHER: Oh, he's only about 500 yards away. Ask for his captain. The name is Künsterlich.

FATHER: Right. (*He goes over to the telephone.*)

The MOTHER *goes out. The* NEIGHBOR *starts tuning his violin.* CATHERINE *looks around her.* JACQUES *gets up and stretches.* MARIE *describes a few dance steps by herself in the middle of the room. The* FATHER *claps his hand over the telephone receiver and calls out to the* NEIGHBOR:

Pipe down, you silly old fool. I can't hear a word he's saying! . . .

Violent explosion, prolonged stuttering of machine guns. The FATHER *speaks over the phone, unhurriedly, then hangs up. The noise dies down.*

He's coming right away. The captain is sending him over in a few moments. They've got another three yards to cover and that's it. Their overtime will be up then.

CATHERINE: How are they doing?

FATHER: I don't know. From what he says, things seem to be going all right.

JACQUES (*uninterested*): For whom?

FATHER: Oh, for both sides, I suppose . . . For the Americans and for the Germans. The captain's rather vague, but he sounds optimistic.

The MOTHER *enters, followed by* CYPRIENNE.

Oh, good, here's my eldest daughter! . . .

CYPRIENNE *allows herself to be embraced.*

You've arrived at just the right moment. I hope you're in good form?

CYPRIENNE: Of course I am.

MOTHER: We've got a surprise for you—your fiancé will be here any minute. You can open the ball with him.

FATHER: You see how hard we're trying to do everything to make you happy.

CYPRIENNE: Then how about finding me a different fiancé while you're about it?

FATHER (*laughs loudly*): Ho! ho! You little devil, you! . . . You know you're just longing to marry your Heinz!

CYPRIENNE *nods agreement with an air of disgust.*

NEIGHBOR: I can't think what's gone wrong with my fiddle—I can't change the speed on it any longer. (*He starts manipulating a small lever on the violin. Sharp explosion.*) Ah! . . . Now it's working! . . .

FATHER: You gave us quite a scare.

JACQUES: Can you play "Little Brown Jug"?

NEIGHBOR: No. I don't know that one. I only like American songs.

JACQUES: All right, then, play "Sweet Adeline."

NEIGHBOR: Sorry, I only know things like "Swanee River" and "Sweet Sue."

MOTHER: Do *all* American songs begin with an S?

JACQUES: Of course not, mom, don't be silly.

MOTHER: Sorry.

NEIGHBOR: What's he doing, that fiancé? He'd better

hurry up and get here while my fiddle is still working.

Sound of knocking at the door.

ALL: Ah! Oh! That's him! At last! . . .

Enter two SISTERS OF CHARITY.

FIRST SISTER OF CHARITY: For the poor of the parish . . .

SECOND SISTER OF CHARITY: If you please . . .

ALL: Grrr! . . . Grrr! . . . (*They hurl themselves upon the* SISTERS OF CHARITY *and throw them out.*)

FATHER: What nerve! Especially on a day like this.

Sound of knocking at the door. Dead silence.

Come in!

Enter HEINZ *and his* CAPTAIN. *Both shy and blushing. They salute in unison.*

HEINZ: Hello, Marie.

CYPRIENNE: Hello, Heinz. You have to call me Cyprienne from now on.

HEINZ: Oh yes? Hey, have you hurt your hand?

CYPRIENNE: It's nothing. I've been opening cans of food.

HEINZ (*bitterly*): American K-rations, no doubt.

CYPRIENNE: No, darling. Just cans of beets. (*She goes up to him and kisses him.*)

General relaxation.

CATHERINE: So you are Cyprienne's fiancé?

CAPTAIN KÜNSTERLICH: May I say a few words?

FATHER (*affably*): Please carry on, Captain. Children, allow me to present to you Captain Künsterlich.

Smiles, nods and greetings.

Well, well, Captain, is everything all right over in your sector?

CAPTAIN KÜNSTERLICH: That's exactly what I wanted to mention. The fact is, things aren't going too well . . .

FATHER: Tut tut! When we spoke on the telephone just now, you seemed quite happy about the situation.

CAPTAIN KÜNSTERLICH: Things have changed since then. At that time I only had eleven casualties among my entire strength of a hundred and twenty men. Now, suddenly, I don't know what happened, but there's only myself and Heinz . . .

MOTHER: Oh dear, so Heinz's comrades in arms won't be able to come to his wedding?

CAPTAIN KÜNSTERLICH: I am really terribly sorry, madam, but I'm very much afraid that Heinz cannot get married just at the moment. Heinz, my old friend Heinz! . . .

HEINZ *hides in* CYPRIENNE'S *arms.*

FATHER: But why?

CATHERINE: It really doesn't matter if his fellow soldiers come or not.

CAPTAIN KÜNSTERLICH: Oh, it's not that, it's just that if

I don't have *any* soldiers left under my command, how can I go on being a captain?

MOTHER (*soothingly*): Well . . . does it really mean so much to you, being a captain?

CAPTAIN KÜNSTERLICH: It does carry a measure of respect, you know. Now then, Heinz, say good-by to these ladies and gentlemen, and come and help me look for our field telephone. It's all we have left. Those Americans are busting up absolutely everything. (*Suddenly noticing the presence of* JACQUES.) Excuse me. No offense meant.

JACQUES *shrugs. No one speaks. The* CAPTAIN *realizes that the general atmosphere is becoming increasingly hostile. He retreats slowly, in the direction of the trap door. Stage business involving the* NEIGHBOR, *who has got hold of the lever working the trap door, lifting it when the* CAPTAIN *gets further away from the edge.*

Surely you understand the delicacy of my position. (*To the* MOTHER:) Madam, please don't look at me like that . . . It's not my fault that the other hundred and nineteen are dead. Be reasonable . . . I must have at least one soldier, mustn't I? Now don't be cross with me, please . . . At least, show me a little understanding, won't you? . . .

During this speech, CATHERINE *has been looking everywhere for a hammer. She finds one, sidles up to the* CAPTAIN *and hits him on the head with it. He falls straight into the pit, the* NEIGHBOR *having lifted the trap door just in time.*

CATHERINE: Right, come on, all of you. We'd better get them married right away. Mama, run off and start preparing the wedding banquet. (*She looks at her watch.*) If we all pull our weight now, we'll have everything ready on time and we'll be able to get the whole affair settled once and for all.

JACQUES: I'll be right back. (*He goes out.*)

MARIE: I'm going up to put on my false eyelashes. (*She goes upstairs.*)

MOTHER: Heinz, Cyprienne, come and help me gather the eggs.

They go out.

You others can set the table . . .

Enter ANDRE.

CATHERINE: Oh, there you are, André. We're running short of women, the way things are going. Go and dress up as a girl.

ANDRE: You must be mad! . . . Oh, no . . . Absolutely not!

CATHERINE: Oh, but absolutely yes . . . (*She gives him a long, hard look.*)

ANDRE *goes out. The* FATHER *draws himself up and studies her enormous bosom admiringly.*

FATHER: There's no doubt about it, Catherine, you're well stacked up front!

NEIGHBOR (*tapping his forehead*): Which is more than one can say about her father!

FATHER (*sharply*): That's quite enough from you, you dirty old man. Give me a hand getting the meal ready. Catherine, will you spread the tablecloth?

CATHERINE: But, dad, the table is covered with junk!

FATHER: Well, get rid of it all, then. (*To the* NEIGHBOR:) Hey, you, clear the table instead of standing there twiddling your thumbs.

NEIGHBOR (*grumbling*): I never did learn to twiddle my thumbs, so how can you accuse me of that? (*He tries surreptitiously to twiddle his thumbs.*)

FATHER: Are you still at it? (*He slaps the* NEIGHBOR's *hands.*) I told you to clear the table.

NEIGHBOR: Oh, go f . . .

Glare from the FATHER.

. . . freshen up a bit, for goodness' sake. Look at your bristles! Your daughter's getting married, you know. (*He goes up to the table, picks up a plank and uses it to scrape things off the table.*)

FATHER: That's it, get down to it, both of you!

NEIGHBOR: You know something? I haven't seen any English soldiers around here.

FATHER: Of course not. This is a landing, not an evacuation.

CATHERINE *brings along a tablecloth.* ANDRE *comes in, dressed as a girl. He is sniveling.*

ANDRE: Why did you make me dress up like this, Catherine? I feel silly. Just look at me!

CATHERINE: Not at all, you look sweet.

Silence. The table is now set. There are flowers in the center, with an enormous knacker's plane as centerpiece. At each place setting is positioned a horse-head skull with a napkin between its teeth.

ANDRE: Catherine, can't I at least change back into my own shoes? With these high heels, I trip every time I try to take a step.

NEIGHBOR: Practice, for pete's sake! It's no more difficult than walking the tightrope! . . .

ANDRE: But I don't know how to walk the tightrope, either.

CATHERINE *shrugs her shoulders. Silence.* ANDRE *gets up, tries to walk and crashes to the floor.*

Oh, shit . . .

FATHER: Come on, hand over your shoes, I'll fix them.

ANDRE, *still sitting on the ground, takes his shoes off and gives them to the* FATHER *who fixes a large piece of wood to each sole, then hands them back.*

ANDRE: Do you really think they'll be better like that? (*He puts them on, starts walking and catches one foot in the other. Another tumble, even more acrobatic than the previous one. He stays on the floor, looking glum.*)

NEIGHBOR: Well, I'm off to take a leak. (*He goes out.*)

CATHERINE *keeps coming and going, setting the table.*

FATHER: Just watch how you go, Jacqueline.

ANDRE *pays no attention.*

Do you hear what I say?

ANDRE: But . . . You're talking to *me*?

FATHER: Of course. I can hardly call you André when you're dressed like that—it would be like talking to a pansy, and I can't stand that sort of thing.

ANDRE (*grief-stricken*): Nor can I. (*He gets up as best he can.*)

Sound of knocking at the door. Enter the GERMAN SOLDIER *who appeared at the beginning of the play to deposit his weapons so that he could run faster.*

GERMAN SOLDIER: Good day, sir. (*To* ANDRE:) Good day, miss. (*To the* FATHER:) You recognize me, ja?

FATHER: Nein.

GERMAN SOLDIER: This morning I left a rifle, a bazooka, and some other things here. May I take them away again now, ja?

FATHER: If you can find them. They've probably been tidied away.

GERMAN SOLDIER: I see you are setting the table to celebrate the great event, ja?

FATHER: When one's daughter gets married, one has to bring out the best china, even at the risk of a few breakages.

GERMAN SOLDIER: Ah, ja, ja. In the words of our Japanese allies: "The strength of China is its weakest chink." (*He laughs silently at his own joke.*)

FATHER: Were you expecting to stay? There doesn't seem to be much space left . . . (*He looks anxiously toward the pit.*)

GERMAN SOLDIER: I do not want to get in the way of your preparations (*he glances at* ANDRE *who lowers his eyes and blushes*) . . . but I'd be glad to stay, thank you, sir.

FATHER: Only if you dress up as a girl. Then you can help Jacqueline finish laying the table.

GERMAN SOLDIER (*disappointed*): Oh! Is she a boy?

FATHER: Of course he is! Do you think I can't get young men to act as hired helps just as efficiently as women?

GERMAN SOLDIER: Hmm! Excuse me, please, but I must rejoin my unit, ja ja, there are only ten of us left out of a hundred.

FATHER: Sorry to hear that. Well, pass by later on, if you like. Do you know Heinz?

GERMAN SOLDIER: Certainly I do.

FATHER: Then do drop in to say hello to him. I know he'd like that. (*He looks into the pit.*)

GERMAN SOLDIER: But what about all my weapons, sir? Are they still here, ja?

FATHER: I don't know. Have a look in the yard.

The GERMAN SOLDIER *goes out.* CATHERINE *continues setting the table.*

ANDRE: The others are certainly taking their time.

FATHER: You're never satisfied. Like this, you've plenty of time to set the table.

ANDRE: My stockings won't stay up.

FATHER: Well, fasten them to something, then. Can't you even dress yourself at your age?

ANDRE: Yes, I can dress myself, but my breasts keep on dropping down too . . .

FATHER: Hold them up with a string around your neck. That's what your mother does.

Enter HEINZ *and* CYPRIENNE.

FATHER: Did you find those eggs you went out for?

HEINZ (*bad-tempered*): I'm certainly not getting down on my knees, scrabbling around for nonexistent eggs. To hell with it all! The Americans are here, let them take care of the birds!

CYPRIENNE: Heinz, you're not going to be in a bad mood, today of all days?

HEINZ: Well, really, it's a bit much. We've been here for four years, and suddenly a mob of foreigners arrives on the scene and nabs all the local produce.

FATHER: What's the matter with him? Doesn't he want to get married after all?

CYPRIENNE: Heinz, please, do cheer up.

HEINZ: And who, may one ask, is this female here?

ANDRE: Hey, come off it, Heinz, do you mean you don't recognize me?

HEINZ *shrugs his shoulders.*

FATHER: You can call him Jacqueline if you want, it suits him better.

HEINZ: Just typical! You French have this mania for disguising yourselves all the time. Why can't you simply wear uniforms like the rest of the civilized world?

CYPRIENNE: Heinz! Sweetheart! Be nice to my dad, please.

HEINZ: I tell you, I wash my hands of the whole affair. What's the point in wearing oneself out for years on end, trying to set a country on its feet again, looking after the people, helping them, when a bunch of strangers suddenly takes over and steals all the eggs. From now on, I'm going to be on the receiving end. And, come to that, when do we eat?

FATHER: We must wait until Jacques gets back. He went to find a priest, and that may take him a little while. There isn't one for miles around.

HEINZ (*sarcastically*): Oh, don't wory about that. I'm quite sure the Americans would never land anywhere without a flock of chaplains in tow. (*He stretches himself and yawns.*)

Enter the NEIGHBOR.

ANDRE: Please may I go and change back into my own clothes?

FATHER: Look here, Jacqueline, just shut up, will you?

CATHERINE: Heavens above, surely you can go on wearing your dress just to please your father?

FATHER: Anyway, you nitwit, the local priest wears a skirt, too, but you don't hear him complain.

NEIGHBOR: Although he did tell me yesterday that it was a darned inconvenient costume for climbing trees . . . Well, shall I play you something on my fiddle to help pass the time?

Sounds of knocking at the door. Enter JACQUES, *puffing and sweating. He makes a sign for someone to come and help him.*

JACQUES: André!

ANDRE: What?

JACQUES: Come and help me! To bring in my crates!

ANDRE: That's not suitable work for a lady.

NEIGHBOR: I'll give you a hand if you want.

JACQUES: Please.

They go out and return lugging a large heavy crate.

NEIGHBOR: My God, it's heavy!

They go out and fetch in a second crate, depositing both crates somewhere on stage out of sight of the audience.

JACQUES: There's still a third crate to come in. I'll go and get it.

FATHER: What's inside these?

JACQUES: An army chaplain. Dismantled. I'll go and bring his clothes in. You can start opening up the crates.

The FATHER *and* ANDRE *get tools and approach the crates, while* JACQUES *goes out, returns with a smaller crate and joins them. The* MOTHER *joins them, followed by the* NEIGHBOR *who has, meanwhile, been trying to repair his violin with strips of adhesive tape.*

MOTHER: Where did you find him, Jacques?

JACQUES (*putting down the third crate and turning to his* MOTHER): Oh, the beach is littered with crates: they are giving them away to anyone who asks for one.

HEINZ (*in a bantering tone*): You American forces *do* seem well organized. I imagine we can all just sit back and take it easy now. (*He looks at* JACQUES, *who puffs himself out with pride.*)

JACQUES: I selected a jumbo-size, fully automated, brand-new model.

CATHERINE: Clergymen, Coca-Cola, and Cadillacs—that's just about what it amounts to, your western democratic system. And all those imbeciles outside are bashing each others' faces in for *that*! You may as well leave your chaplain unassembled, for all the use he'll be!

JACQUES: Oh, he'll be useful all right. He's equipped with radar.

CATHERINE: A fat lot of good that will do him! (*She laughs contemptuously.*) One of our big guns will soon finish him off!

MOTHER: Now then, Jacques. Come now, Catherine, stop

provoking your brother. (*To the* FATHER:) Listen, why don't you stop putting that gadget together and come and have lunch. I think it might be better if we had the banquet before the wedding is consummated—I mean, consecrated . . .

FATHER: Cyprienne, call your sister.

CYPRIENNE: Yes, dad. (*Going to the door.*) Marie, chow's up. (*She returns.*)

MOTHER: Take your places, all of you. Jacques, you sit on my left.

As JACQUES *goes toward the table,* CATHERINE *puts her foot out and trips him. He falls to the floor with a crash, gets up again, takes off one of his shoes and hurls it at Catherine's head. The shoe misses her and goes through the window. The* MOTHER *continues to seat her guests.*

Cyprienne . . . on my left; Heinz . . . euh . . . on my left; and the Neighbor . . . mmm . . . on my left. All the others, sit on my left.

They all go up to the table and sit down.

FATHER: Listen, Marie, since Marie isn't down yet I may as well finish putting the chaplain together. It's not fair, leaving him at the bottom of the crate like that, with his guts in the air and his legs unscrewed. It worries me.

He walks over to the crates and finishes assembling the CHAPLAIN *who appears suddenly, looking rather dazed, in uniform, with small crucifixes in his jacket lapels. Meanwhile the following conversation takes place between the* NEIGHBOR *and* JACQUES.

NEIGHBOR: Do you have any port? I like a glass of port before my meal.

MOTHER: No, only sweet vermouth. (*Holding out a bottle.*)

NEIGHBOR: Ah no! None of *that* brand. The director of that firm is a Protestant.

JACQUES: Do you hold anything against Protestants?

NEIGHBOR: Yes, a grudge.

JACQUES: May one ask why?

NEIGHBOR: Their priests don't wear neckties.

JACQUES: Well, neither do you for that matter. Why don't you join the Protestants yourself?

NEIGHBOR (*considering this suggestion*): Good lord! I never thought of it like that . . .

JACQUES: Anyhow, you're boring the ass off me!

NEIGHBOR: Hey, Jacques, now you're going too far! (*He brandishes his violin and brings it down over Jacques' head. It smashes into smithereens, and he looks at it mournfully.*) Darn it! Now I'll have to start repairing it all over again. (*He walks over to the workbench.*)

FATHER (*coming forward with the* CHAPLAIN): May I introduce the Reverend . . .

He turns questioningly toward the CHAPLAIN, *who*

searches through his pockets and finally finds a small piece of paper which he unfolds.

CHAPLAIN: Taylor . . . Robert Taylor . . .

CYPRIENNE: Oh! . . . It's Robert Taylor. (*She rushes forward and tugs at his sleeve.*) Come and sit down beside me.

JACQUES: What's going on? I must have chosen the wrong crates. (*To the* CHAPLAIN:) Are you really an army chaplain?

CHAPLAIN: Certainly I am.

JACQUES: Excuse me . . . it's your name . . . I don't quite understand . . .

CATHERINE (*sneering*): That's American civilization for you. Propaganda, propaganda all the time. They not only send us chaplains, they give them film stars' names. And you fall for that! Ugh! You make me sick, the whole bunch of you!

NEIGHBOR: Hah! That's the stuff. (*To the* CHAPLAIN:) Do you get the same rations as the G.I.'s?

CHAPLAIN: No. We hold a rank equivalent to lieutenant or captain, depending on our age. Entitlement to six bottles of whisky a month. (*He looks at his glass and addresses* JACQUES:) Would you look in the second crate? There should be a bottle of whisky somewhere in it.

CYPRIENNE: Would you give me your autograph? Are you still married to Barbara Stanwyck?

NEIGHBOR (*rushes up to* CYPRIENNE): Brothel bait! Daughter of a whore!

HEINZ (*aside, after glancing at* CYPRIENNE): I wish she was a Jew. Ah, those Jewish girls . . . (*A nostalgic sigh.*) Sarah, dear Sarah! I got a thousand marks for turning her in. (*A sigh of regret. A contrast must be made between the first sigh, of nostalgia, and the second sigh, of regret. On the latter occasion, he shakes his head mournfully.*) And I've spent it all.

JACQUES: Reverend sir, do you not think it might be more appropriate to join these two in holy matrimony right away, rather than wait until after lunch?

MOTHER: But what's the hurry? We've got plenty of time afterward.

Enter MARIE, *wearing a very chic and revealing dress —the latest Paris fashion.*

CATHERINE: Ah, there she is at last! About time, too.

Up till now, no one has sat down at the table, except the MOTHER *who has been looking at them one after the other, and* CYPRIENNE, *who has been continuously getting up and sitting down again, while staring wide-eyed at the* CHAPLAIN.

MARIE: What's the matter? I wasn't lost. Did you know there were three Americans upstairs?

CATHERINE: I can well believe it. They seem to be everywhere.

HEINZ: Just like cockroaches. Those Yanks are as bad as us Jerries. (*He laughs.*)

FATHER (*filling the glasses*): Here, Reverend Taylor, let me serve you first.

CATHERINE: Ha, ha. Just wait till he finds out what he's drinking!

CYPRIENNE: Listen, Catherine, why don't you stop teasing us all? We're enjoying ourselves. And after all, it's not you who's getting married, it's me!

NEIGHBOR (*coming up to the table, brandishing his shattered violin*): It's beyond repair.

CATHERINE *punches a passing glass so that the contents spill all over* JACQUES. *The glass flies through the air and smashes noisily on the ground. All get up from their seats.*

CATHERINE: Why don't you go over to your crates and find another glass, since this one is so fragile?

JACQUES *empties his own glass down her neck.*

Revisionist! Running dog of capitalism! Vile deviationist! Imperialist stooge! Illegitimate offspring of a Trotskyite ape!

FATHER (*severely*): Catherine, I don't know if you were taught that kind of language at the Kremlin, but really . . .

CATHERINE *hurls herself upon* JACQUES. *They roll about on the floor.*

MOTHER: Hey, you two! Catherine! Jacques! Will you stop this at once! (*She takes a jug of water and pours it over the two combatants. They both jump up, furious.*)

CATHERINE: It's all Jacques' fault.

MOTHER: Catherine, leave your brother alone.

CATHERINE: We didn't need Jacques here to help Cyprienne marry Heinz . . . (*She delivers a straight right to Jacques' chin.*)

JACQUES: Mama! . . .

MOTHER: Oh, go on fighting for all I care. (*To the* FATHER:) Do come and sit down. (*To the* CHAPLAIN:) Please sit down, sir. Cyprienne, make your guests sit down.

JACQUES *and* CATHERINE *sit down.*

NEIGHBOR (*to the* CHAPLAIN): After you . . .

CHAPLAIN: No, no, after you, please . . .

FATHER: Who's going to say grace? I don't care so much for myself, but no doubt it would give you pleasure . . .

NEIGHBOR (*brandishing his violin*): Ah, it's working again. (*The handle snaps.*) Oh, bugger it! (*He goes over to the workbench, bangs his violin down on it, then comes back.*) I'll say grace, if you like.

CHAPLAIN: Hold on, we'll choose someone this way. (*He counts around the table.*) Eeny—meeny—miney—mo—catch—a—froggy—by—the—toe—when—he—hollers—let—him—go—eeny—meeny—miney—mo. (*By cheating, he ends up with the* NEIGHBOR.) Up to you, sir.

NEIGHBOR: Oh! Well, I think we'll skip it just this once. (*He sits down.*) I wouldn't mind a glass of that sweet vermouth.

CHAPLAIN: That's better. You're coming around at last.

MARIE: Ma, may I kiss the reverend gentleman? Since my fiancé hasn't turned up?

MOTHER: Marie! (*Bursts into tears.*) Now I have no children left at all! . . .

FATHER (*to the* MOTHER): Come now, Marie, calm down. By the way, do you know what I found under the bed this morning?

MOTHER: No, my God, what was it?

FATHER: Dust.

MOTHER: You scared me.

FATHER: I was scared too. I thought it was a man.

MOTHER: Oh, shut up with your feeble jokes.

CHAPLAIN: This vermouth is delicious.

FATHER: I make it myself from the horse bones I find when I clean out the pit with the scraper.

CHAPLAIN: Really? (*He takes a sip.*) A little more, please.

The FATHER *serves him.*

NEIGHBOR: Ha ha! You didn't put him off after all! Think you're clever, eh? (*He holds out his glass.*)

FATHER: And you? (*Pour himself what remains in the bottle.*)

The NEIGHBOR *looks annoyed.*

MOTHER: A little mackerel, Reverend Taylor?

NEIGHBOR: Go on, take some. He'll probably tell you he caught it himself.

FATHER: Of course I caught it. Stands to reason. (*He offers the can of fish to the* CHAPLAIN.) But I can't remember just when.

NEIGHBOR: How do you recognize it now that it's canned?

FATHER: I always tag their tails after I've caught them. Look, here's the tag!

CHAPLAIN: A little salt on this particular tail, please.

CATHERINE: You just wait. You'll soon find yourself digging more salt than you need in our Siberian mines.

The MOTHER *passes him the salt.* CATHERINE *snatches it away before it reaches him.* JACQUES *hurls himself on her.*

FATHER: Are you two out of your minds, fighting like that while you're at the table?

CATHERINE *has knocked* JACQUES *down, and now returns quickly to her place.*

CATHERINE: Pass me the mackerel. (*She helps herself, then returns to the battle.*)

MARIE (*in a superior and languid voice*): I say, mother may I join in the fight?

During the whole brawl, the combatants exchange occasional brief interjections such as: "Bastard!," "Lousy slob!," "Bitch!," "Slut!," etc.

FATHER (*to the* MOTHER): Marie! Pass the chicken to the Reverend.

CHAPLAIN: It looks delicious. A little breast, please: that's the part I like most.

MOTHER: André, you can sit down and eat now.

The two combatants stumble back against the workbench, which collapses.

NEIGHBOR: Good grief! My fiddle! (*He rushes over, picks up the violin from the debris and returns to the table.*)

CATHERINE (*getting up and glaring at the* CHAPLAIN): Well, here I am fighting because of you, and you sit there chewing chicken, you petty-bourgeois reactionary! Do you think the revolutionary struggle will cease simply because you ignore it?

CHAPLAIN: But . . . euh . . . I didn't ask you to start fighting. And, anyhow, as you say, you are fighting because of me, not for me. A slight difference! . . .

CATHERINE: Right, get to work!

She pulls him to his feet and hurls him into the battle, that is to say on top of JACQUES *who is just lifting himself painfully off the ground. Howls of pain from* JACQUES.

JACQUES: Hey, Reverend, let go of that . . . ouch! . . . that's my foot! . . .

CHAPLAIN: I don't give a damn. To hell with all of you. (*He sits up for a moment.*) Is my make-up foundation still nice and smooth?

CATHERINE *gives him a straight right to the jaw and*

he collapses. CATHERINE *leaps into the air triumphantly before falling on the prostrate pair.*

MARIE (*bouncing up and down in her chair with excitement*): Oh, ma, let me join in!

CYPRIENNE: Let her have a go, ma, please, since she's so keen. I want everybody to have a good time on my wedding day.

MOTHER (*turning to the* FATHER): Should we let her?

FATHER: Look, I really couldn't care less. (*To the* NEIGHBOR *who is pouring himself a drink:*) Hey, you miserable old skunk, are you going to leave some for me?

HEINZ (*tenderly*): My Cyprienne . . . (*Wheedlingly.*) Give me a little chicken.

NEIGHBOR (*examining his violin carefully*): Those bastards have buggered it up for good.

He hurls himself into the battle. At this moment, the CHAPLAIN *emerges from the group. The* NEIGHBOR *smashes his violin over the Chaplain's head. The latter looks up, rubs his head and returns to the fray. The* NEIGHBOR *steps back to aim a blow at him, misses, overbalances and falls flat on his face, knocking himself out.*

FATHER: Am I right in thinking that Captain Künsterlich is still in the pit?

HEINZ: Yes. I haven't seen him since he fell in.

Loud explosion outside.

MOTHER: That's the last straw. Now they're beginning to kick up a din again. I can't even marry off my daughter in peace and quiet. Just think, if we had invited any friends along! . . .

NEIGHBOR (*suddenly sitting up*): Aren't I a friend?

FATHER: Yes, but we didn't invite you.

The NEIGHBOR *relapses into his coma.*

CHAPLAIN: Let go of my leg! . . . Ow! Ooh! Let go of my leg! . . . A hundred days of indulgences if you let go of my leg. Ouch! (*Furious.*) You goddam son-of-a-bitch, will you let go of my leg or not?

He gets a judo hold on JACQUES *and hurls him into the air.* JACQUES *comes down on his feet, whirls around like a top and falls into the pit. A terrible sound of clashing metal emerges.*

HEINZ: What a strange sound! You must have left Captain Künsterlich still wearing his medals.

FATHER: Yes, so I did. I'll go and have a look. (*He gets up, turns around and goes over to the pit.*)

At this moment, the combatants fall against the table which collapses in a tremendous clatter of breaking dishes. MARIE *jumps up, takes off her shoes and leaps into the fray.*

MARIE: Oh, I just can't wait any longer.

MOTHER: Jacqueline, help me to set the table straight.

ANDRE *helps her. The* FATHER *comes back, shaking his head. He picks up a plate, sits on the floor and starts eating.*

CHAPLAIN: Holy Mary Mother of God! Help me in my hour of need! Let go of me, you female lunatic!

He struggles free, hotly pursued by MARIE, *stumbles and falls into the pit.* MARIE *leaps into the air, then lands straight on top of him in the pit, emitting a bloodthirsty yell.*

HEINZ: That's divine punishment for having annoyed other people.

ANDRE: May I go and change now?

FATHER: Aren't you comfortable like that, Jacqueline? You know, you'll have far more success with the Yanks if you stay as you are.

ANDRE: I'd rather put my pants back on and have no success at all. In any case, I don't like having a cold breeze blowing around my bum.

The NEIGHBOR *and* CATHERINE *are by now both stretched out cold on the floor.* HEINZ *and* CYPRIENNE *are having a quiet grope in the background. The door opens to admit the older of the two Resistance Leaders,* VINCENT.

VINCENT (*optimistically*): Here I am again!

FATHER: Isn't the Colonel with you?

VINCENT: No, he's in bed, his mother won't let him out after curfew.

FATHER: Ah! Like a bite to eat?

VINCENT: No, thanks. We've been thinking. I've come to requisition your Rollswagen after all. In wartime one can't be too fussy.

FATHER: Oh, I quite agree! Mustn't be fussy. Go out that way (*pointing in the direction of the pit*), and do drop in any time.

VINCENT *disappears into the pit.* CATHERINE *staggers to her feet, loses her balance and follows* VINCENT *into the pit.*

Marie, is there any of that potted mackerel left?

MOTHER: Yes. Here it is. (*She takes the plate, goes up to him and breaks it over his head, then, clutching her heart, totters over toward the pit and falls in.*)

ANDRE: I think I'll take this chance to go and change back into . . . (*He tiptoes out.*)

HEINZ *and* CYPRIENNE *are by now engaged in increasingly heavy petting. After a few moments, enter the Chorus of* FOUR SOLDIERS (*the two* AMERICAN SOLDIERS *and the two* GERMAN SOLDIERS.) *This time they are dressed in Salvation Army uniform. They group themselves around* HEINZ *and* CYPRIENNE *and sing "I Love You Truly" in barbershop quartet style.*

FATHER (*to the* NEIGHBOR): Hey, you old fool . . .

The NEIGHBOR *stirs vaguely, lifts himself on to his elbows, groans.*

Do you feel better?

NEIGHBOR (*holding his jaw*): Not too bad. (*He spits out a mouthful of teeth.*) Did everything go off all right?

FATHER: Did *what* go off?

NEIGHBOR: The wedding.

FATHER: Well, you were there, weren't you? You saw it all?

NEIGHBOR: No. (*Pause.*) Where's my fiddle?

FATHER: Oh, no dancing at the moment, please, I'm feeling a bit tired. We'd better do a bit of tidying up around here. And then back to work, I suppose. I wonder what happened to my plane?

NEIGHBOR: Good idea. I think I'll go and see if everything's all right over at my place.

Sound of knocking at the door. HEINZ, CYPRIENNE *and the* FOUR SOLDIERS *slowly climb the stairs in procession.*

NEIGHBOR *and* FATHER (*together*): Come in!

Enter two French officers, a CAPTAIN *and a* LIEU-TENANT.

FATHER *and* NEIGHBOR (*in unison*): Good day, gentlemen.

CAPTAIN: Does this house belong to you? (*He inspects the incredible disorder.*) Well, you're lucky. You've got off pretty lightly here.

FATHER *and* NEIGHBOR (*in unison*): Ah?

LIEUTENANT: You should see the rest of the town.

FATHER *and* NEIGHBOR (*in unison*): All knocked flat?

The two officers nod their heads.

CAPTAIN: I have some bad news for you. And some good news immediately afterward.

FATHER *and* NEIGHBOR (*in unison*): I'd rather hear the good news first.

CAPTAIN: Well, to start with, then, you are liberated.

NEIGHBOR (*delighted*): Yes? (*He springs to attention, notices that the* FATHER *is not following his example, and quickly resumes his usual slouch.*)

FATHER: What else?

CAPTAIN: And then . . . (*He stops, embarrassed.*)

FATHER: Go on, don't be shy.

CAPTAIN: Well . . . (*He hesitates, then adopts an official tone of voice.*) I must first of all inform you that I represent the Ministry of Reconstruction.

The FATHER *listens glumly.*

In this capacity . . . hmm . . . I am concerned with the Plan of the Future . . . (*He goes to the door and makes a signal.*)

Enter THREE SAPPERS* *armed with axes.*

All right, men, carry on. I've explained the matter tactfully to the owner.

LIEUTENANT (*explaining*): You see, your house is standing in the way of our future project. It's out of line.

FATHER: Well, that's the first I've heard of that.

The SAPPERS *are scurrying around shifting furniture and lugging in cases of dynamite.*

CAPTAIN (*takes the* FATHER *by the arm and walks him over to the door, waving his arm demonstratively*): Now, out there will stretch, in the future, a great

* See Translator's Note, p. 105.

vista lined with Japanese poplars. Pleasure gardens and ornamental fountains will enhance the beautiful scene. Flowering plants and bushes will waft their perfume on the breeze.

LIEUTENANT (*going up to the* SAPPERS): Ready? All right, let's go, then.

They all run out. The SAPPERS *light the fuses and get out too. Total blackness descends on the scene, followed by a shattering explosion. Red glare. Blackness again. When light returns, the stage sets have vanished. A backdrop depicts weed-covered ruins. Piles of debris in the foreground. The* CAPTAIN *and the* LIEUTENANT *are seated by the side of the* FATHER, *who appears to be dead. The* NEIGHBOR *lifts up the father's head, then lets it drop again.*

CAPTAIN (*getting up*): Bah! You can't make an omelette without breaking eggs.

NEIGHBOR (*seizes the Captain's revolver and shoots him with it*): I quite agree. (*He then fires at the* LIEUTENANT *who kills him with a shot from his own revolver.*)

LIEUTENANT: Vive la France! . . .

The "Marseillaise" suddenly blares out, abominably out of tune. The LIEUTENANT *draws himself up proudly and marches off, doing the goose-step.*

END

(which, by a happy chance, coincides with that of the play)

Translator's Note

The author points out, in a footnote to the first published edition of the play, that at the original performance at the Théâtre des Noctambules in 1950 the exigencies of the small stage made it technically impossible to end the play as written. Consequently, the three Sappers were replaced by a "charming Boy Scout" who announced himself with the words: "Scout of France, always prepared, my heart on my sleeve." And the curtain went down at the Lieutenant's order to the Boy Scout to light the fuse of the dynamite he had just brought in.

An Evergreen Original (E-458) $1.95

THE KNACKER'S ABC
(L'Equarrissage pour tous)
A play by Boris Vian
Translated by Simon Watson Taylor

In this play, the horrors of world catastrophe are presented with what Cocteau called "an exquisite insolence." **The Knacker's ABC,** a paramilitary vaudeville, takes place on June 6, 1944, during the landing of Anglo-American forces at Arromanches. In the midst of complete chaos, the sole concern of the horse knacker and his family is the problem of their daughter's marriage to a German soldier who has been billeted in their house. The grimness, cruelty, and idiocy of our contemporary world is thoroughly exposed by Vian's deft use of the absurd. In addition to the text, this volume includes an introductory note by Jean Cocteau and a Preface by Boris Vian in which he discusses his intentions in the play and the difficulties of the first production.

"...the concept of fighting war by means of war, as some choose to do, seems to be quite intolerable, and there remains, alas, only a limited choice of alternative methods... The play is above all a burlesque: it seemed to me that the best approach to war was to laugh at its expense, a craftier but more effective way of fighting it...."

—Boris Vian

Boris Vian died in 1959 at the age of 38. As novelist, poet, and playwright, he had little success during his lifetime with the publication of his works and the production of his plays. As well as a writer, he was a singer, composer, jazz trumpeter, translator, and engineer. Today his literary reputation has grown to such a degree that he is currently one of the most popular writers in France. His works are being translated into a dozen languages. This is the third Vian play to be published in America — the others being **The Empire Builders** and **The Generals' Tea Party.** Three novels are planned for future publication by Grove Press.

GROVE PRESS, INC., 80 University Place, New York, N.Y. 10003